# THE 'Q' SQUAD

An habitual criminal attempts to snatch Penelope Hayes' handbag, yet is apprehended and charged. Two months later, she's abducted and chloroformed — and again rescued by the police. This time her assailant escapes with her handbag. It seems that the wave of daring criminal gang robberies across London is somehow connected to Penelope's handbag — despite her denials that it contained anything of value. Then she disappears again — and the police have a murder investigation on their hands . . .

Books by Gerald Verner
in the Linford Mystery Library:

THE LAST WARNING
DENE OF THE SECRET SERVICE
THE NURSERY RHYME MURDERS
TERROR TOWER
THE CLEVERNESS OF MR. BUDD
THE SEVEN LAMPS
THEY WALK IN DARKNESS
THE HEEL OF ACHILLES
DEAD SECRET
MR. BUDD STEPS IN
THE RETURN OF MR. BUDD
MR. BUDD AGAIN
QUEER FACE
THE CRIMSON RAMBLERS
GHOST HOUSE
THE ANGEL
DEATH SET IN DIAMONDS
THE CLUE OF THE GREEN CANDLE

GERALD VERNER

# THE 'Q' SQUAD

*Complete and Unabridged*

**LINFORD**
*Leicester*

First published in Great Britain

First Linford Edition
published 2012

British Library CIP Data

Verner, Gerald.
  The 'Q' Squad.- -(Linford mystery library)
  1. Detective and mystery stories.
  2. Large type books.
  I. Title II. Series
  823.9'12–dc23

ISBN 978–1–4448–1367–8

Published by
F. A. Thorpe (Publishing)
Anstey, Leicestershire

Set by Words & Graphics Ltd.
Anstey, Leicestershire
Printed and bound in Great Britain by
T. J. International Ltd., Padstow, Cornwall

This book is printed on acid-free paper

To

MY FRIEND

VINCENT LAWRENCE

WITH EVERY GOOD WISH

# 1

## The Girl in the Charge Room

Sub-Inspector Arnold Lake came into the charge room at Meadow Lane police station and nodded to the desk sergeant.

'Good evenin', sir,' said that grizzled man. 'The Super had to go out but he left a note for you.'

He searched among the papers at his elbow and produced an envelope. Arnold Lake took it, slit it open with his thumb, and hastily read the contents.

He was a pleasant-faced man, whom some people called good-looking. Straight of back and keen of eye, with hair that was so fair that it was only after a second glance that the grey at the temples was noticeable, and belied his youthful appearance. He might have passed for twenty-five but was in reality ten years older than this.

His thin lips pursed as he finished

reading the message, and he looked up at the desk sergeant.

'I'm sure this bunch have got their headquarters in the neighbourhood all the same, Fisk,' he said. 'Twice I've traced them after a job to this area, and each time lost 'em somewhere in the district.'

He was referring to a new gang of 'smash-and-grab' thieves that had recently made its appearance, and succeeded in getting away with a surprising quantity of jewellery, the results of a series of raids on suburban jewellers' shops.

'It's more'n likely, sir,' agreed Sergeant Fisk, removing his steel-rimmed spectacles and breathing on them carefully. 'This district's pretty bad, but you know that without me tellin' you.'

Arnold did know that. Deptford is one of the worst areas for crime. The majority of the inhabitants are a lawless lot, born and bred into thievery and worse. In the maze of mean and narrow streets behind Meadow Lane live men and women whose occupations are best not enquired into too closely, and who seldom venture forth from their dirty hovels until after the light of day has faded from the sky.

Here the police patrol in couples, and woe betide the unwary stranger who, by accident, finds his way into this haunt of the pick-pocket and the bag snatcher, for he will be lucky to emerge without a 'bashing' and the loss of all his portable possessions.

This is the real underworld so glibly written and talked about, compared to which Limehouse is a model village.

'I've been here for fifteen years,' continued the desk sergeant, polishing his glasses vigorously with his handkerchief, 'an' I've seen an' heard things that'd make your blood run cold. They ain't 'uman, some of the people round here, and to call 'em animals is flatterin' 'em.'

Arnold nodded. He also had seen and heard things.

'They got a feller in Grape Street the other night,' went on the sergeant, peering through the lenses at the lamp on his desk. 'I don't know what he'd done, but six of 'em set on him — with broken bottles. His own mother wouldn't have known him when our chaps found him and took him to hospital. He died the next day, and I reckon he was lucky.' He sighed, fixed his glasses on his broad nose and shook his head. 'An in'uman lot of brutes,' he said. ''Anging's too good for 'em.'

'And yet every time we hang one of them there's a demonstration against capital punishment, and we're accused of legalised murder,' said Arnold.

The sergeant sniffed disparagingly.

'Not by anybody with any sense,' he grunted. 'Only hysterical women with more money than brains who want to see their pictures in the papers, and can't think of any other way to get talked about. Are you goin' to wait for the Super, sir?'

The young inspector shook his head.

'No,' he answered. 'I must be getting back. I've got a conference at the Yard.'

Sergeant Fisk regarded him enviously.

'If I was a younger man I'd like your job,' he said. 'But there weren't no 'Q' cars and Flyin' Squads when I was your age.'

'There weren't any motor car crooks

then,' pointed out Arnold truthfully. 'It's not all fun, though, being in the 'Q' Squad.'

'I'll bet it's more fun than sittin' behind a desk,' said the sergeant, 'taking down charges against drunks, an' sneak thieves — '

He broke off, his head on one side listening.

'Sounds as though another was just comin' along,' he grunted.

In the silence that followed Arnold could hear the measured tramp of feet from outside, and presently, in confirmation of the sergeant's prophecy, a policeman entered, grasping a thin-faced, shabbily-clad, man by the arm.

The man he recognised, but his eyes were fixed on the girl who followed close behind. Slim, grey-eyed, red lipped. Mentally he catalogued her attractions. Expensively dressed, too. The coat she was wearing was real mink; the smart little hat a Paris model. Arnold, who understood such things, wondered at her presence in Meadow Lane. The females of that district were flamboyant when they were not drab. Certainly this girl did not belong. There was an air about her that radiated West End.

The policeman had marched his charge up to the desk.

'I was on duty on Tanner's Hill when I saw this man snatch this lady's handbag and make off with it,' he said in the sing-song voice which policemen adopt for such occasions. 'I chased him and took him into custody.'

He laid a handbag on the desk.

'What's your name?' asked Sergeant Fisk, eyeing the shabby little man.

'You know it well enough,' answered the prisoner. 'Martin.'

'Address?' said the sergeant, writing laboriously in his book.

'Eleven Grape Street,' growled the other sullenly.

The station sergeant looked over his glasses at the girl.

'Is this lady makin' the charge?' he asked.

'Yes.'

The girl answered for herself, and Arnold thought he had seldom heard a sweeter voice.

'What's your name, Miss?' said the sergeant.

'Penelope Hayes,' she answered. 'I suppose you want my address as well?'

'If you please,' said Sergeant Fisk. 'Just a moment while I get the name down. Now, Miss.'

'The Park Hotel, Knightsbridge.'

As she gave the address Arnold wondered what had brought her so far afield.

The sergeant wrote it down carefully and blotted it.

'You'll get a notice when this feller comes up for trial, Miss,' he said, and turning to the constable: 'Search him, Miller, and put him in the cooler.'

The policeman ran his hands scientifically over the thin faced crook, and then the formalities of charging him were completed.

'Too bad, 'Cosh',' said Arnold, speaking for the first time. 'I thought you were still in prison.'

'Cosh' Martin, so called because he had twice been convicted for robbery with violence, swung round, and his lips

7

curled back from his yellow teeth in a snarl.

'Oh, it's you, is it?' he growled. 'What you doin' snoopin' round, eh? You'll get yours one day.'

'It'll take a cleverer man than you, 'Cosh',' said Arnold. 'And you won't have much chance for the next four or five years. The last time you were brought before the magistrate you were warned that if you came up again it would mean a stiff sentence.'

'I wasn't thinkin' about me,' snarled 'Cosh' Martin, licking his lips, 'or hooks like me. You watch out, Mr. Clever Dick. There's a feller comin' what'll put paid to a lot of you 'busies.' Serve yer damn well right.'

'You sound almost interesting,' remarked Arnold. 'Who is this wonderful man?'

'Just you wait and see,' grunted 'Cosh.' 'Even your old boxes of tricks won't help you.'

Arnold smiled at this slighting reference to the 'Q Squad' cars.

'You can laugh,' growled the little crook, 'but you'll be laughin' on the other side of your face in three moons time — if you're alive.'

'What's going to happen in three months' time?' asked Arnold, but 'Cosh' Martin apparently thought he had said enough, for he relapsed into a sullen silence and refused to answer any further questions.

He was taken to the cells, and the girl, who had been listening interestedly, looked at the sergeant.

'Can I go now?' she asked.

That grey-haired man nodded.

'Yes, Miss,' he answered.

'And I should advise you to leave this vicinity as soon as possible, Miss Hayes,' put in Arnold. 'It's not very healthy, particularly after dark.'

She smiled a little ruefully as she picked up her bag.

'I think you're right,' she said. 'Is there a cab rank near here?'

Arnold shook his head.

'The people round here don't go in for cabs,' he replied, and seeing her dismay: 'I'm going Westward, if you wouldn't object to travelling in a police-car I should be pleased to take you with me.'

After the slightest hesitation she accepted his offer, and, saying goodnight to the station sergeant, Arnold escorted her out to his waiting car.

At sight of that ancient looking vehicle she raised her eyebrows, and guessing her thoughts, Arnold chuckled.

'It doesn't look exactly like a Rolls, does it?' he said. 'And it's not intended to. That's camouflage, Miss Hayes. That old-fashioned body conceals one of the finest engines made.'

She was quickly to have proof of his assertion. Once they were clear of the narrow streets he let the car out, and heard the girl beside him gasp.

'And that's only a half of what it can do,' he boasted. 'So you see, you should never go by outward appearances, particularly with a 'Q' car.'

'I've read about Scotland Yard's mystery fleet,' she said, smiling, 'but I never thought I'd ride in one.'

At her request he reluctantly set her down at Trafalgar Square.

'Thank you, Mr. — er — ' She paused

enquiringly, and Arnold hastily supplied his name — 'Mr. Lake,' she went on. 'It was nice of you to give me a lift. Good night.'

'Good night,' said Arnold, releasing the small, gloved hand she had given him.

He watched her cross the road and disappear up Pall Mall. Rather regretfully he turned the car and ran slowly down Whitehall.

Penelope Hayes. A pretty name and a pretty girl. What had she been doing in Tanner's Hill? It had been on the tip of his tongue to ask her more than once, but he had thought better of it. After all, it was none of his business. He would probably never see her again.

Shrugging his shoulders he dismissed the girl from his mind, and entering the Yard made his way to the conference room, where two weary Chief Constables were awaiting him.

Two months later he was to meet Penelope Hayes once more, in circumstances that nearly cost him his life.

# 2

## The 'Nose'

'Cosh' Martin was sentenced to five years as an habitual criminal, and left the dock a man with a grievance.

'Is there sich a thing as justice?' he complained bitterly. 'Fancy that old so-and-so givin' me a five stretch. And it wasn't even my idea to snatch the girl's bag. I was paid to do it. It's the feller what paid me you want.'

'What's his name?' asked the unimpressed detective, to whom he confided his wrongs.

But Mr. Martin was vague. He had met the man at a public-house on the previous evening. A short, fat fellow with a sandy moustache. He'd never seen him before, but they had got friendly over a drink. The other had put forward his suggestion. He had described the girl minutely. Said that she would be at Tanner's Hill at nine o'clock the following night. If Mr. Martin could get away with her bag there would be ten quid waiting for him, plus whatever money the bag contained.

The sceptical sergeant listened to the story and sniffed.

'You've been reading fairy tales,' he said.

'It's the truth!' protested 'Cosh' Martin indignantly, 'as sure as I'm 'ere.'

'Well, the 'beak' didn't believe you, so I don't see why I should,' retorted the sergeant, and locked the tale-spinner up in a cell pending his transfer to Pentonville.

'Cosh' Martin had served six weeks of his sentence when the rumours began to reach Scotland Yard. They trickled in from various areas, but mostly from such hot-beds of crime as Notting Dale, Tidal Basin and Deptford. Divisional Superintendents received the reports from their subordinates and with worried frowns passed on the information to headquarters.

The Assistant Commissioner called a meeting of the four Chief Constables who each control one of the four areas into which Greater London is divided.

'Something's brewing,' he said gravely, looking at the grey-haired men seated at the table in the conference room. 'During the last month a wave of excitement appears to have spread among the criminal classes. From the various reports that have come in it looks as though an attempt was being made to organise all the smaller crooks quartered in and around London.'

Chief Constable Cranley, a thin-faced, dour man, smiled sceptically.

'You're not suggesting, sir,' he protested, 'that a criminal organisation is being formed? Such a thing has never been heard of outside the pages of one of these crime novels.'

'I'm not suggesting anything,' said the Assistant Commissioner a little testily. 'I'm merely informing you of what is taking place.'

'I've heard some of these rumours,' remarked a stout and pleasant-faced man named Tilman, who had been wounded in the notorious battle of Sydney Street, 'and I certainly agree that something curious is going on.'

'But this 'master criminal' stuff,' grunted Cranley shaking his head, 'you're not considering anything like that seriously, surely?'

'Why not?' asked Tilman, looking at him steadily.

'Because it's outside all police experience,' retorted Cranley. 'Nothing of the sort has ever happened before.'

'Because it's never happened before is no reason why it shouldn't be attempted,' said the Assistant Commissioner quietly. 'And from the reports which have reached me certainly something of the sort is taking place.'

Cranley shrugged his broad shoulders.

'I'm not disputing that there may be one or two local gangs being got together,' he said. 'That sort of thing happens all the time. But anything wholesale is, in my opinion, out of the question.'

He was supported in this assertion by the two men who had not as yet spoken, but the Assistant Commissioner was not convinced.

'Well, something very unusual is happening,' he declared. 'You have only to glance at a précis of these reports that have come in for confirmation of that. And, in the public interest a close watch must be maintained. Any signs of systematic organisation must be checked at once, and the ringleaders arrested.'

The conference continued until late in the afternoon. When it finally broke up the four Chief Constables went away to their different offices to arrange for a general tightening up of the administration of the area for which each was responsible.

Arnold Lake was the first to discover anything definite about this underworld unrest. Belonging to the mobile force, which embraces the 'Flying Squad,' and head of Scotland Yard's sixteen 'Q' cars — those mysterious machines which, disguised as trade vans or decrepit saloons, possess the finest engines made, and are capable of bringing a rapid concentration of men to the locality of a suspected crime — he was less restricted than his confrères to certain districts.

The rumours which were worrying his superiors had reached his ears before they had become the subject matter for the lengthy reports that were trickling into Scotland Yard, and in truth, a large percentage of these reports had originated in his discoveries.

There was a man called Ernie Williams who supplied Arnold with a lot of out of the way information. The 'nose,' or police informer, is regarded by all classes of society with disgust and loathing. Lawful and lawless alike look upon him with scorn and detestation. His company is shunned. His career, once the nature of his profession is discovered, is generally of the shortest duration. Even Scotland Yard is not in sympathy with the 'squealer,' though it does not hesitate to make use of him. More criminals are caught by 'information received' than by any other means.

No one among the people he mixed with suspected Ernie Williams of being a 'nose,' but there was many a man who had spoken incautiously in front of him, who was now pacing a prison cell, and wondering, with bitterness, who had betrayed him to the police.

The skinny figure of Ernie Williams was a familiar one in the Deptford district. He was undersized and painfully thin, with stooping shoulders and an unpleasantly sallow complexion that extended to his large and pendulous nose. His hair was black and lank and looked as though it was permanently wet. Even on the hottest day he wore a shabby overcoat that had originally been made for a man of larger build, and draped around his bony form with no pretensions of fitting.

His origin was obscure. He had appeared in Deptford three years before, and none knew from whence he came or anything about him. And no one bothered. For some time, being a stranger, he was regarded with an element of suspicion, but this gradually wore off as his shuffling figure became a familiar object in the district.

On a night when a thin fog hung over Meadow Lane and its surrounding mean streets Arnold Lake picked up the little 'nose' in response to a telephone call he

18

had received earlier in the day. Ernie Williams was waiting at the corner of the deserted street, and swung himself aboard the 'Q' car as Arnold brought it snailing along the sidewalk.

'Get out of this district as soon as you can, Mr. Lake,' he muttered, as he settled himself beside the young inspector.

'What's the matter, Ernie?' asked Arnold quickly, glancing at his passenger sideways, for Ernie William's small eyes were looking nervously into the foggy darkness of the street.

The 'nose' shook his head.

'I don't know,' he whispered hoarsely. 'There's somethin' big on foot and I'm scared. Get out of this neighbourhood and I'll tell you what I know.'

Arnold obeyed, driving through New Cross into Brockley and on in the direction of Forest Hill.

'Now,' he said, as he swung out of Brockley Rise into Stanstead Road, 'spill it.'

Ernie Williams licked his thin lips, and his shifty eyes darted this way and that.

'There's somethin' doing,' he said

huskily. 'All Deptford's in an uproar, and there's a whole bunch of new crooks being smuggled into the district.'

'What do you mean — smuggled?' asked Arnold sharply. 'Where from?'

'From all sorts of places,' replied the 'nose,' lowering his voice, though it was impossible for anyone to overhear him. 'They've been arrivin' from all parts of the world for the last few weeks. 'Slim' Harris is 'ome from Australia. 'Bud' Ludlow drifted over from Chicago three days ago, an' there's a heap of fellers trickled across from the Continent. They make their way to Deptford at night, and then they disappear. They're hidden away in basements and kept out of sight.'

Arnold was interested. This information tallied with the other rumours that were going about.

'What's at the bottom of it all?' he said.

Ernie Williams shook his head.

'I don't know,' he answered. 'I'm tryin' to find out. It's my idea that some Big Feller's tryin' to form a gang — '

Arnold laughed incredulously.

'You've been reading books, Ernie,' he

accused, but the little man was serious.

'You can laugh, Mr. Lake,' he said earnestly, 'but I'm telling you the truth. These fellers are all actin' under somebody's orders.'

'Whose?' demanded Arnold.

Williams rubbed his long nose and gave an expressive twitch to one of his skinny shoulders.

'Yes, whose?' he muttered. 'That's what I want to know. I've only got to mention the subject and everyone shuts up like oysters. I can tell you this, though, whoever the feller is he's powerful.'

Arnold stared at the road ahead. There came to his mind the words of 'Cosh' Martin. Was this what the bag-snatcher had hinted at in the charge room at Meadow Lane Police Station?

Ernie Williams had no more information to offer, and Arnold dropped him at a bus stop at Brockley.

On his way back to the Yard the young inspector was very thoughtful. Absurd as it seemed, what he had learned that night tended to confirm the fact that some kind of criminal organisation was being attempted. But who was responsible? Among the known crooks Arnold could think of no one capable of carrying through such a gigantic undertaking. He never guessed that the secret had been within his reach that night in the charge room at Meadow Lane when Penelope Hayes had had her bag snatched, for in the girl's bag had lain the answer to his question.

# 3

## The Bank Robbery

It was on a Saturday evening two weeks after Arnold's interview with Ernie Williams that Scotland Yard received its first practical confirmation of the rumours which had brought worried frowns to the foreheads of its administrators.

A City policeman placidly patrolling the deserted length of Lombard Street had been surprised to see a white-faced and agitated man come flying out of the main entrance of the Westland Bank. He recognised him at once for the manager, and listened aghast to the incoherent story that was told him.

Following its usual custom the bank had closed its doors at twelve o'clock, the staff remaining to finish up the overflow of the morning's work. That morning two hundred thousand pounds in paper currency had arrived from the Bank of

England and had been put in the vault for distribution on the Monday to the Westland Bank's various provincial branches. The manager had been signing letters in his private office when he had been overcome by an attack of faintness, and remembered nothing more until he recovered consciousness some five hours later. Feeling sick and ill and wondering what had happened, he had staggered out into the main room of the bank, to find the entire staff in a similar condition to himself.

Realising that his own experience had not been due to natural causes his thoughts had instantly flown to the money stored in the vault. Searching for his keys he found, to his horror, that they had disappeared, and in a panic, accompanied by the Chief Cashier, he had made his way down to the vault to discover the huge door wide open and the two hundred thousand pounds gone.

The amazed policeman went back with him to the bank and telephoned to the headquarters of the city police in Old Jewry. From there they relayed the information to Scotland Yard, and a few minutes later a squad of City men and detectives from Central Office arrived at the Westland Bank and took possession of the premises.

The method by which the staff had been overcome and the robbery carried out was soon discovered. For the past week a gang of workmen, swung in cradles above the street, had been cleaning the front of the building of its coating of grime and soot, using the flexible steam pipes with which such operations are carried out. Instead of finishing early they had come back at one, the foreman explaining that they would be working overtime in order to complete the contract by the scheduled date.

'It's easy to see what happened,' grunted a big inspector. 'They substituted some kind of gas for the steam and put the nozzles of the hoses through the open windows, floodin' the interior of the bank and puttin' everyone to sleep. Clever!'

'But,' gasped the agitated manager, 'the contractors are a reputable firm. They surely wouldn't lend themselves to — '

'I don't suppose for a moment they know anythin' about it,' broke in the C.I.D. man, and he was right.

After some difficulty the manager of the firm was found and questioned. He had no knowledge of any overtime being put in on the bank job. He supplied the address of the foreman who had been in charge of the work and this man was interviewed at his home in Kennington. His statement tallied with that of the manager. He and his men had finished for the day at one o'clock and had not come back.

'It's obvious,' said a City Superintendent, rubbing the side of his nose, 'the men who came back were the robbers. It was a pretty ingenious plan, and I'll take my hat off to the man who thought of it. These fellows were seen by three policemen, but naturally were never suspected.'

The bank was searched from vault to roof, but no clue likely to lead to the identity of the robbers was found. They had carried out their job efficiently and disappeared, none knew whither. A constable had seen a heavily-laden saloon car pass him in Gracechurch Street just before four, but being unsuspicious had failed to note the number. He was a man interested in cars, however, and was able to give an accurate description of the machine. It had been travelling Westward.

'It may or may not have contained the people we're after,' said a Scotland Yard inspector dubiously, 'but it's worth trying to trace it.'

A telephone message was put through from the Yard to Imber Court, in Surrey which houses the wireless installation, once at the top of Scotland House. Twenty minutes later every 'flying squad' car and 'Q' car were called and a description of the suspected saloon issued in morse.

Arnold Lake, cruising leisurely along East India Dock Road, was notified of the happening by his wireless operator.

'Blue Daimler Saloon, eh?' he grunted. 'I should think it's miles away by now or hidden up.'

He came through Poplar and Stepney into Aldgate. The City, when he reached

Fenchurch Street, was deserted except for an occasional policeman and one or two caretakers out for an airing. Crossing London Bridge he began to work back on the South side of the river towards Bermondsey, and eventually found himself running by Southwark Park towards Deptford.

He had seen many cars on the road, but few blue ones, and none that answered the description of the suspected Daimler. Neither did he expect to. The people who had been clever enough to get away with two hundred thousand pounds from the Westland Bank would not be such fools as to overlook the fact that the machine might have been seen and its description circulated. By now it was most probably housed in some obscure gagage in whatever district the thieves had made for. This was always supposing that the Daimler seen by the constable had anything to do with the robbery at all. There was no certainty that it had.

Going slowly along Evelyn Street Arnold saw a taxi approaching from the direction of High Street. It was getting late and taxis were rare in that district. He glanced at it curiously as it passed. The next second he uttered an exclamation and his foot came down on the brakes as he brought the 'Q' car to a halt.

The light from a street lamp had illumined the interior of the cab, giving him a momentary glimpse of a white-faced girl struggling desperately with a man who was trying to force something he held in his hand over her mouth. But that instant's vision had been enough for Arnold to recognise Penelope Hayes!

With a word to the wireless operator in the back he swung the car round. The street was too narrow to turn in one movement and he had to back the machine before he could face in the opposite direction. By the time he had done this the cab was turning the corner into Redriffe Road.

With a bound the 'Q' car shot forward in pursuit. The taxi had increased its speed, and slowing to take the corner Arnold saw that it was already some distance ahead, but its engine was no match for his, and so swiftly did his machine eat up the distance between them that the cab might have been standing still.

As he drew level with it the driver looked round with a scowl, and then seeing that the 'Q' car kept alongside he uttered an oath.

'Go on,' he snarled. 'Don't take up the 'ole bloomin' road, pass if you're goin' to!'

'I'm not going to!' snapped Arnold grimly. 'Pull your cab into the side of the road and stop!'

'You go to Hell!' growled the driver truculently. 'What's the game?'

'There's no game,' retorted Arnold. 'This is a police car and I'm an inspector of the Mobile Branch.'

A pencil of flame darted from the interior of the taxi and a bullet hummed wickedly past his head. The second shot grazed his ear and smashed the windscreen, and before a third could be fired Arnold pressed hard on the accelerator and the car leaped ahead.

'Get out as I come to a stop and blow your whistle!' he shouted to his companion, and as that astonished individual removed his headphones he gave a twist to the wheel and pulled the car up broadside in the path of the speeding taxi.

As he opened the door and sprang out he heard the scream of brakes as the driver tried frantically and vainly to avoid a collision. The bonnet of the cab crashed into the side of the stationary car and coincident with the impact came the shrill blast of a police whistle as Arnold's wireless operator carried out his instructions.

The young inspector ran round to the taxi, expecting another fusillade of shots, but apparently the driver and the shooter had decided to give up the contest, for he saw that they had scrambled out of the damaged cab and were running up the street. Arnold went after them. He was a better runner than they were, and he was gaining when the man with the gun stopped suddenly, swung round, and fired two shots at almost point-blank range. An agonising pain caught him in his left ankle and with a gasp he stumbled and fell.

By the time he had picked himself up the two fugitives had disappeared down a side turning.

A hasty examination of his ankle showed him that the wound was not a serious one. The bullet had cut a thin gash across the bone, and although it was bleeding profusely it was nothing to worry about. Improvising a bandage with his handkerchief he limped back to the interlocked cars.

Two policemen came running up as he reached them and Arnold hastily explained what had happened. He cut this as short as possible and went painfully over to the taxi. The interior reeked of chloroform and the girl was lying back in one corner of the seat, her eyes closed and her face chalk white. She was unconscious, but whether this was from the effects of the drug or because she had fainted from shock there was no telling.

'We'd better get her along to Meadow Lane Station,' said Arnold. 'Lift her into my car, will you?'

The two policemen obeyed and the limp form of the girl was put in the back. Arnold got in beside her and his wireless operator took his place at the wheel.

After some manoeuvring the 'Q' car was extricated from the smashed front of the taxi and leaving the policemen to guard that damaged machine they drove to Meadow Lane.

Sergeant Fisk looked at Arnold in surprise as he limped into the charge-room.

'Hello, sir!' he said. 'Met with an accident?'

'Yes,' replied Arnold grimly. 'I came into collision with a gunman.'

The desk sergeant's eyebrows shot upwards, but Arnold checked the flood of questions that hovered on his tongue.

'I've got Miss Hayes in my car,' he said, 'and she's unconscious. Send somebody out to bring her in, will you? And let the matron look after her.'

It was a night of surprises for the sergeant. His eyes opened wide, but he said nothing, pressing the button on his desk. Giving an order to the constable who answered the summons, he watched interestedly while the man went out, and with the help of the wireless operator brought in the still unconscious form of Penelope Hayes.

She was taken through to the back of the station and handed over to the care of the police matron, and only when this had been done did Arnold give the desk-sergeant an account of what had occurred.

'First she has her bag snatched and then somebody tries to kidnap her,' said Sergeant Fisk, shaking his head. 'That girl seems to attract trouble, sir.'

Arnold was thinking the same. This last affair had, however, been much more serious than 'Cosh' Martin's bag-snatching effort. Arnold had been unable to be present when the little thief was brought up for trial, but he had heard of the excuse which 'Cosh' had put forward, and, like everyone else, disbelieved the story of the unknown man who had offered ten pounds for the girl's handbag. In view of this night's incident, however, he was inclined to change his mind. Had 'Cosh' Martin been speaking the truth after all? It certainly looked like it.

The voice of the desk-sergeant broke in on his thoughts.

'I don't like this shootin' business, sir,'

said the grey-haired man dubiously. 'There's somethin' un-English about it.'

'I didn't like it either,' said Arnold truthfully, for those bullets had come unpleasantly close.

'These fellows are pretty bad round here,' went on the sergeant shaking his head, 'but they've never taken to carryin' guns before. If they're goin' to start that Lord 'elp us!'

Arnold said nothing. He was tired and his ankle was paining him severely. But for his interest in the girl and the hope that she would be able to supply a reason for the attempted abduction, he would have been on his way home long ago.

Sergeant Fisk noticed his white face, and looked sympathetic.

'I'll bet that foot of yours is hurting like Hell,' he remarked. 'If I was you I'd — '

What he would have done had he been Arnold was never destined to be known, for at that moment the pleasant-faced police matron put in an appearance.

'The young lady's recovered consciousness,' she announced, 'and she wants her handbag.'

'Handbag?' said Arnold frowning. 'Have you seen it, Sergeant?'

The sergeant shook his head.

'No, sir,' he replied. 'You didn't bring it in.'

'Perhaps it's in the car,' said the young inspector, hobbling to the door. 'I'll ask my operator.'

But that individual had seen no handbag, and was prepared to swear that there had been no handbag in the taxi when the girl had been lifted out. He was a family man and had particularly looked.

'That gunman must have taken it with him,' said Arnold curtly, and followed the matron through the door at the back of the charge-room to interview Penelope Hayes.

# 4

## Penelope's Story

The girl lay on a truckle-bed in the little apartment that the police matron used as a duty room. The pallor of her face was startling, but she essayed a smile as Arnold came in.

'So I'm here again,' she said weakly.

He nodded.

'And very fortunate you are to be here,' he answered gravely. 'But for a piece of extraordinary luck I think you would have recovered consciousness in a much more unpleasant place.'

She shivered.

'What exactly happened?' she asked, and he told her as much as he knew.

'The man got in at the corner of High Street,' said Penelope, when he had finished. 'He was waiting on the pavement and the driver slowed up. I thought he was going to enquire the way, but the man wrenched open the door, sprang in, and before I knew quite what had happened was trying to press that filthy cloth over my face.'

She shivered again, and for a second the fear of that moment came back to her eyes.

'Where did you pick up the taxi?' asked Arnold.

'In Brompton Road,' she replied, and then, as she saw the curious look on his face, 'I thought I should be safer in a cab.'

'From what?' he said sharply.

She hesitated.

'From — from anything,' she answered lamely. 'My last experience had warned me that this district was dangerous.'

'And yet you came here again?' Arnold looked at her steadily. 'Why did you come to Deptford tonight, Miss Hayes?'

'I — I have a friend living here.' She avoided his eyes as she spoke. 'Well, not exactly a friend but — an old nurse. I came to see her. I do visit her occasionally.'

'Surely it was rather late for a visit?' He raised his eyebrows.

She made no reply, and he went on after a pause.

'Where does your — er — this old nurse live?'

'On Tanner's Hill,' she answered promptly. 'I don't know the number, but I know the house by sight.'

'I see.' Arnold unconsciously pursed his lips. 'And was that where you were going when 'Cosh' Martin snatched your bag?'

She nodded.

'Do you know any reason for this attempt being made to kidnap you?' he continued.

'No.' There was a slight delay before she replied, and she looked a little uncomfortable. 'Why are you asking me all these questions?'

Instead of answering he put another question.

'Was there anything very valuable in your bag, Miss Hayes?' he enquired.

'No,' she said shaking her head. 'There was a little money — three pounds and some silver, but that was all.'

'It hardly seems worth the trouble and risk,' he remarked, and saw her eyes fill with dismay.

'Why? Do you mean — did they — '

'They got it this time,' he broke in. 'The man who tried to drug you must have put it in his pocket when he ran away.'

She was, he thought, unnecessarily upset at his information, and her appearance only went to confirm his conviction that she was keeping something back. It was absurd to suppose that the loss of three pounds odd could have brought that look of worry to her face. There was something besides that in the bag — something that was so valuable to these people, whoever they were, that they were prepared to go to any lengths to obtain possession of it.

She must have seen something of what he was thinking in his face, for she pulled herself together hastily.

'Well, they didn't get much for their trouble, did they?' she said. 'I don't mind losing the money, Mr. Lake, but the bag itself was — was a present. It has a sentimental value. I wouldn't have lost it for anything.'

This sounded plausible, but Arnold was

under the impression that she had thought of the explanation on the spur of the moment. The man in the cab had not only been after the bag, he had been after Penelope Hayes as well. That was obvious. If the bag had been the only object there was no need for the chloroform. He could easily have jumped into the taxi, snatched the bag and jumped out again, without having recourse to the drug. However, if the girl refused to speak it was impossible to force her. He asked a final question.

'Would you recognise this man again?' he said, 'the man who got into the taxi in the High Street?'

She shook her head.

'No,' she answered. 'I don't think I would. It was dark and he wore a muffler over his mouth and chin.'

The matron came in at that moment with hot coffee, which Penelope welcomed eagerly, and Arnold went back to the charge-room.

Ringing up Scotland Yard he reported the incident to an interested inspector.

'We ought to be able to get the driver,

anyhow,' said that official when Arnold had given the number of the cab. 'I'll have him looked up in the register.'

He rang off, and Arnold glanced at the clock. It was twenty minutes past twelve. As soon as the girl had recovered sufficiently to leave the police station he could drive her back to her hotel, or at least to some point where it would be easy for her to pick up a taxi, and after reporting at the Yard seek the rest he was craving for.

A constable came in with a jug of coffee and Arnold accepted a cup of the scalding fluid and drank it gratefully. He had just finished it when the telephone bell rang and Sergeant Fisk called him to the instrument.

'Headquarters wants you,' he said briefly.

It was the inspector to whom he had spoken a short while before.

'That cab of yours was stolen late last evening from outside an eating house in Tottenham Court Road,' said the inspector. 'The driver reported his loss at half-past nine. The cab itself belongs to the Fleet Taxi Company. They've got about a hundred on the streets and their garage is in Waterloo Road.'

Arnold made a grimace into the mouthpiece.

'So there's no clue at all to the two men who were with it?' he said.

'None whatever,' grunted the inspector, 'unless that girl can recognise them again.'

'She can't,' said Arnold. 'I've asked her.'

He hung up the receiver and went to enquire how Penelope was feeling.

He found her sitting on the edge of the truckle-bed powdering her face with a puff borrowed from the matron.

'I'm quite all right,' she said, in reply to his question.

'I'm terribly sorry to have given you so much trouble.'

'You haven't given me any trouble at all,' said Arnold, and suggested that he should drive her back to the West End.

She smiled.

'This is the second time you've had to take me home,' she said.

'And I hope it will be the last,' replied Arnold fervently, and reddened as she raised her eyebrows. 'I didn't mean it exactly like that.' He stammered in his confusion. 'What I meant was I hope . . . you won't come here any more . . . ' He realised that this was worse, and became incoherent.

This time she laughed outright.

'It doesn't sound very complimentary,' she said, 'but I don't think you mean to be rude.'

He was apologising all the way to the car.

Because of his wounded ankle he sat beside her in the back during the journey, and although she was willing enough to talk she would say very little regarding herself.

He gathered that she had lived most of her life abroad, for she confessed that she had only been in England for a little over six months. But when he tried to draw her out to talk more about herself she grew reticent.

He took her as far as Hyde Park Corner, and as she said goodbye became suddenly bold.

'May I call tomorrow and see how you are?' he asked.

She looked at him speculatively.

'If you promise to make it an unofficial visit,' she said, and her eyes danced. 'I'm not going to answer any more questions.'

'I won't ask any,' he promised, and she nodded.

'I'll be in about four,' she said, and with a parting smile left him.

He watched her cross to a cab rank and step into a taxi. As it moved off she waved and Arnold reentered the 'Q' car feeling absurdly pleased with himself. Mystery or no mystery, the girl held an attraction for him that no other woman had ever equalled. Already he was wishing that it was four o'clock on the following afternoon, when he would be seeing her again.

Still thinking of Penelope Hayes, he arrived at Scotland Yard to find that grim building in a ferment of excitement, for during the last hour news had come through that fourteen jewellers' shops in various parts of London had been broken into, and property to the value of over three-hundred-thousand pounds stolen.

# 5

## The Garage

About half way along Waterloo Road on the right hand side stands a large building the arched entrance to which abuts on a side street. Day and night a ceaseless activity goes on behind the high wall that encloses the large paved courtyard, lit after dark by hissing arc lamps. For this is the headquarters of the Fleet Taxi Company, and through the wide gates come and go the black and red cars that during the past two months have become so familiar on the streets of London.

The Fleet Cabs created something of a sensation when they first appeared. Never before had anything approaching their comfort and luxury been available to the public at the ordinary taxi hire charge. Their highly polished paintwork and chromium fittings, their leather upholstery and smooth running were more in keeping with a private car than a hackney carriage. The drivers were neatly uniformed, civil, and very ready to oblige. It quickly became a habit for people to wait for a Fleet Taxi sooner than take any other vehicle, preferring the expenditure of a little patience to secure the greater comforts that these resplendent machines offered.

There were other facilities attached to the Fleet Cabs which were not in evidence to the general public. A sensitive microphone had been installed in each one and, cleverly concealed near the head of the driver, was a miniature loud speaker, enabling him to hear every word spoken by the passengers he carried. More often than not the conversation thus overheard was without interest, but several times stray information had been picked up that had proved very profitable to the gentleman who controlled the destinies of the Fleet Taxi Company. For this enterprising organisation served as a cloak to conceal the greatest criminal coterie that the genius and patience of one man had ever succeeded in building up.

To the innocent-looking garage in the Waterloo Road had come by a circuitous route the money so cleverly stolen from the Westland Bank. It had come in broad daylight, concealed under the back seat of one of the company's cabs, and it had passed without suspicion under the eyes of countless watchful policemen, for there is nothing so innocent as a taxi, or any form of vehicle less likely to arouse suspicion.

At a time when Scotland Yard was humming with activity and every reserve man had been called from his bed, a fleet of the black and red taxicabs came gliding swiftly through the silent, almost deserted streets. They came from all parts of London, converging from all points of the compass, to pass at irregular intervals through the high gateway of the garage in Waterloo Road. And in their luxuriant interiors they carried the proceeds of the robberies which at that moment were exercising the best brains of the C.I.D.

In a small square room, furnished plainly as an office, and occupying a position at the back of the garage, Mr. Ely

Sholter, the General Manager of the Fleet Taxi Company, sat at his big tidy desk, a cigar gripped between his yellow teeth, his small eyes fixed on a typewritten list that lay on the blotting pad before him. With a gold pencil he made a tick against the appropriate number on the list as a loud speaking telephone notified him that that particular cab had just returned. There were fourteen numbers in all, and with the exception of two each carried his neat, pencilled, cross beside it.

Mr. Sholter was an unpleasant-looking man. Originally big and muscular, he had run to fat, and his once thick crop of red hair had thinned until it was now but a fringe surrounding the glistening dome of his bald head. His face was sallow, the flesh hanging loosely at the corners of his small mouth and below his chin. There were grey bags beneath his eyes, which testified to the unhealthiness of his life.

Another taxi-cab loomed through the gates of the garage, crossed the spacious square, and coasted down the concrete slope into a huge chamber where many similar vehicles were already ranged.

'Number 1872,' droned the loud speaker, and Mr. Sholter's pencil made a swift dab at the list before him. 'That's the last but one,' announced the telephone. 'Not a hitch up to now. Roughly I should say we've raked in close on three hundred thousand.'

A smile crossed the face of Mr. Ely Sholter and laying down the pencil he leaned back in his chair and rubbed his none too clean hands together complacently. Three hundred thousand pounds! With the two hundred thousand that had been taken from the Westland Bank that made half a million. Not bad for two days' work. And everything had gone smoothly and according to plan. Everything, that is, with one exception!

Mr. Sholter's shaggy red brows drew together as he remembered this item. It had been a great piece of ill-luck that Arnold Lake should have been in the district when Leeman and Conley had succeeded in getting hold of the girl. But for the fact that they had notified him immediately by telephone and he had ordered Conley to report that his cab had been stolen, it might have led to trouble. That was a piece of quick thinking on which he had not yet finished congratulating himself, but it was a thousand pities the girl had escaped. The 'Clever Fellow' wouldn't be pleased at that, and he had a trick of making his displeasure felt.

Mr. Sholter took the butt of his cigar from between his teeth and dropped it into the large chromium bowl beside him. Reaching forward he took another from a box and chewed it thoughtfully. He always referred to his employer as the 'Clever Fellow,' for he knew no other name by which to call him.

His mind went back to that night, four months previously, when, strolling through a quiet street in the West End, the big car had come gliding up beside him and the unknown had called him softly by name. Mr. Sholter had been a little diffident about obeying the invitation to enter that machine, but certain things which the other had told him concerning himself and his business — he was at that time running an unprofitable broker's office in the City — had made him quickly concede to the other's request. For two hours he had been driven round a maze of quiet streets, and during that time had listened to a scheme, the enormity of which had taken his breath away. Who the goggled man sitting beside him was he had no idea, but he quickly realised that he was a genius for organisation, and in the weeks that followed he found no cause to reconsider his first estimate.

'I have the whole plan for this organisation cut and dried,' the unknown had stated, 'and if you decide to accept my offer you will carry it out. Nominally you will be the man in charge, and you will appoint such sub-section leaders as I shall instruct you. But they will report and take their orders from you alone. They will not even know that I exist. You will pay them their salaries and such bonuses as I shall decide on, and for this service you will receive a cash payment of twenty thousand pounds and fifteen per cent of the gross amount we acquire during our activities. I have told you sufficient, I think, to show you what an enormous sum that may be. Now go home and sleep on my proposal. Tomorrow at twelve o'clock I will ring you up at your office and you can tell me whether you are willing to take on the project.'

Mr. Sholter had gone home and slept on the proposal, or rather, to be more accurate, he had lain awake most of the night and considered it. And when at twelve o'clock on the following morning the soft voice of the unknown had reached him over the wire at his office he had made his decision.

'You fully understand that you will only nominally be the head of this concern?' the other had said after his acceptance. 'You will take no initiative, and you will do nothing other than carry out my instructions. Neither,' the voice had continued when Mr. Sholter had signified that he understood this, 'will you now, or at any time, make any attempt to discover who I am. It is doubtful if you would succeed in doing so, but if you did the knowledge would be fatal. I desire no one to know me, and I shall take instant steps to render such knowledge useless. I have no doubt that a moment's thought will tell you what they will be.'

Mr. Sholter's sallow face had paled a trifle, for he was well aware what the other meant.

'Your preliminary instructions will reach you by the first post tomorrow morning, together with the promised twenty thousand pounds,' the unknown had concluded. 'You will obey those instructions to the letter, and when you have carried them out others will reach you in the same way. I shall also keep in touch with you by telephone.'

'Supposing I want to communicate with you?' Mr. Sholter had asked, and the reply had been curt.

'Anything you have to say to me you must say when I ring you up.'

The telephone conversation had terminated, and on the following morning by the first post as promised had arrived a bulky registered packet. Enclosed with the money, the sight of which had brought joy to Mr. Sholter's heart, was a thick wad of closely typewritten instructions. The names of the men he was to get in touch with were carefully set down, and full details regarding the starting and equipping of the Fleet Taxi-Cab Company which was to act as a cover for the nefarious organisation which the unknown's genius was to bring into being.

From the start everything had gone smoothly. The premises in the Waterloo Road had previously been owned by a garage company who were on the verge of bankruptcy, and these people had eagerly accepted Mr. Sholter's offer to take over the place, lock, stock, and barrel. Since it had been used for a similar purpose before, very little structural alterations were necessary, and less than three weeks after his first meeting with the 'Clever Fellow' the Fleet Taxi-cab Company was in full swing. And every one of the huge staff employed was a crook.

Mr. Sholter, staring at the ceiling of his office, his unlighted cigar dancing up and down between his teeth, felt that he was to be congratulated. Only one thing marred his pleasant speculations and that was the girl, Penelope Hayes. The reason why his employer was so anxious to get hold of her was unknown to him. At first it had only been her bag he wanted, but since the unsuccessful attempt by 'Cosh' Martin he had altered his plans, and now his instructions were very definite. It was not only the bag but the girl, too, he wanted now. Well, they'd got the bag and that was something.

'Number 1968,' came the voice from the telephone, to break in on his thoughts. 'That's the lot, Guv'nor, an' all serene.'

Mr. Sholter leaned forward, picked up his pencil and methodically placed a cross opposite the number on his list.

'Have you unpacked the stuff?' he asked.

'All except this last lot,' answered the voice. 'I'm going to do that now.'

'When you've finished come and see me,' said Mr. Sholter, and taking out a box of matches carefully lighted his cigar.

Rising to his feet he went over to a safe in the corner of the office and with a key from his pocket unlocked it. From the interior he took out a lady's leather handbag and stood looking at it thoughtfully.

He had been too busy when Conley and Jake Leeman had brought it to examine its contents, but now that the night's business was practically over he felt curious to know why the 'Clever Fellow' should have been so anxious to get it in his possession.

It was a fair sized bag of the envelope type, and opening the flap Mr. Sholter peered into the interior. It was filled with the usual miscellaneous contents that gravitate into a girl's handbag. There was a handkerchief, a lipstick, a little box of powder and a puff, several letters, and a small purse containing three pound notes and eight shillings in silver and copper. Tucked into a separate compartment was a square envelope. Mr. Sholter pulled this out and fingered it frowning. The flap was stuck down and by the feel of it it contained very little. Was this the reason for his employer's anxiety to gain possession of the bag? There was certainly nothing else in it, unless there was something in one of the three letters.

Curiosity was one of Mr. Sholter's strong points, and he looked at the closed envelope longingly. It was blank and slightly soiled and gave no outward indication of its contents. He would have dearly loved to have opened it, but he was afraid. It might be possible to steam it —

The telephone bell rang softly, and hastily putting the envelope back in the bag Mr. Sholter crossed to his desk and picked up the receiver. The soft, almost whispering voice of the unknown came to his ears.

'That you, Sholter? Did everything go smoothly?'

'Quite smoothly,' answered Mr. Sholter.

'Did you get the girl?' asked the other eagerly.

'No!'

Guardedly, in case the operator at the exchange should be listening, Mr. Sholter explained. The man at the other end uttered an impatient exclamation.

'You must get her!' he said. 'It's important. I'll think of another way.'

'I've got the bag,' said the stout man. 'It's here, in my office.'

'What does it contain?' asked the other quickly. 'Is there a square envelope?'

'Yes,' said Mr. Sholter. 'I don't know what's in it — '

'And you're not to look!' broke in the voice curtly. 'You understand, on no account are you to open that envelope. If you open that it's the last thing you'll ever do.'

'You can trust me,' said Mr. Sholter virtuously. 'I wouldn't dream of opening it.'

'Make the bag up into a parcel,' ordered the other, 'and be outside the Lyceum Theatre in twenty minutes.'

He rang off, and Mr. Sholter hung up the receiver with a sigh. His curiosity concerning the contents of the envelope was not to be satisfied. There was no time now to try his little experiment with steam.

He had just finished making the bag into a rough parcel when there came a tap at the door, and a thin-faced man with grey hair entered.

'Everything put away, Billing?' asked Mr. Sholter.

The under-manager nodded.

'Yes, all shipshape and tidy,' he

announced. He took a key from his pocket and handed it over to the bald man. 'What a haul,' he said, smacking his lips. 'I've never seen so much jewellery before in my life.'

'And you won't see it again,' said Mr. Sholter. 'At nine o'clock in the morning Weinderg will be here to price it and take it away. Have the men gone?'

Billing nodded.

'Most of 'em,' he answered. 'A couple of 'em are having a drink, the last two that came in. The other's have all gone.'

'I'm going myself, now,' said Mr. Sholter putting on his hat and coat. 'I'll be back at half past eight.'

'O.K.,' said Billing. 'D'you want the car?'

Sholter shook his head.

'No, I'll walk,' he answered. 'The air'll do me good.'

The chill of dawn was in the air as he left the garage and walked swiftly in the direction of the bridge. He reached the pillared portico of the Lyceum in just under the twenty minutes stipulated, and he had barely come to a halt before a big saloon turned out of the Strand and drew up by the side walk.

★　★　★

'Get in,' whispered the muffled voice of the figure at the wheel, and Mr. Sholter obeyed.

When he was seated beside the driver the car moved forward, negotiated a side turning and came out into the Kingsway. It traversed that broad thoroughfare and at the top of Southampton Row swung into Russell Square. Here, near the railings of the central garden, the unknown brought the big machine to a stop and broke the silence he had hitherto maintained.

'Give me the bag,' he said, and Mr. Sholter took the parcel from his knees and passed it over.

The driver ripped off the covering with his gloved hands and opening the bag hurriedly searched the contents. He gave a grunt of satisfaction as he found the square envelope. This and the letters he thrust into the pocket of his heavy coat and tossed the bag into the back of the car.

'Now listen,' he said curtly. 'I've thought of a scheme for getting hold of the girl.'

He spoke rapidly for fifteen minutes and when he had finished the tired Mr. Sholter nodded.

'It ought to work,' he said.

'It's got to work!' snapped the other. 'You understand Sholter, there must be no mistake this time. If there's any bungling I shall hold you responsible.'

There was a menace in the soft voice that was unmistakable.

'You needn't worry,' said Mr. Sholter hastily, 'there will be no bungling.'

'Then that's all,' grunted the unknown. 'You can go!'

The big man got heavily out of the car and he had barely reached the roadway before it shot forward and vanished round an angle of the square.

# 6

## Arnold Gets a Shock

Arnold Lake had a small flat at the top of a block of buildings in Victoria Street. It consisted of two tiny bedrooms, a living room, a microscopic bathroom and a kitchen that was probably originally intended for a cupboard and altered only as an afterthought of the architects. It was near to Scotland Yard however, and it suited Arnold's modest requirements.

A pale sun was lacing the streets with yellow light when the young inspector, almost reeling with weariness, inserted his key in the main door and passed into the gloomy vestibule. Closing the door behind him he went over to the small lift and was quickly carried to the top floor. As he let himself into his flat he was greeted by an unmusical snore that came from the smaller of the two bedrooms. Hanging up his hat and coat he crossed the little lobby and turned the handle and looked into the room.

'Wake up, George,' he called, 'and make me some coffee.'

A grunt and a slight movement in the narrow bed was his only answer.

Arnold grinned, and going over shook the sleeper by the shoulder.

'Wake up,' he said again, and with a gasp the man in the bed rolled over and a tousled head appeared. Two small eyes blinked at him resentfully from a thin face.

'Was'er marrer?' enquired Mr. George Seeper huskily.

'There's nothing the matter,' said Arnold, 'except that I want some coffee. Now come along, jump to it!'

His servant sat up with a prodigious yawn and rubbed his eyes. There were people at the Yard who thought, and openly said, that Arnold was mad to employ this man, for at one time Mr. Seeper had been a notorious pick-pocket. But Arnold had never regretted the impulse which had caused him to engage the little crook.

Two years previously, before he had been promoted to the 'Q' Squad, Arnold had arrested Mr. Seeper while his skilful hand was emerging from the pocket of a stout and well-dressed gentleman in a theatre crowd in Shaftesbury Avenue. The little 'dip' had made no fuss, but had accepted his fate with equanimity. On the way to the station he had become confidential and told Arnold something of his life. It was not the usual whining jargon that he was accustomed to hear, and the young inspector — he was a sergeant then — had become interested.

Apparently Mr. Seeper's fall from grace had been more a combination of circumstances than any predilection on his part for thieving. And although he had candidly admitted that he had lived for some time by 'whizzing,' it was not a form of livelihood that appealed to him. He was not an 'habitual,' and when he was brought before the magistrate he received a light sentence. Arnold had a word with him before he was conducted to the cells, and put forward the suggestion which enquiries into Mr. Seeper's story had prompted.

'Would I like to take on the job, sir?' he exclaimed gratefully, when Arnold had asked him if at the end of his sentence he would like to come to him in the capacity of manservant. 'Would a drownin' man like a lifebelt? You bet I would!'

The whole thing had been fixed then and there, and at the expiration of his three months Mr. Seeper had taken up his quarters at the flat in Victoria Street, and for over eighteen months had served Arnold faithfully. He had only one fault, and that was an enormous capacity for sleep. As Arnold said more than once, he must have been born tired.

'I never seem to get enough sleep,' he explained once, 'and the more I 'as the more I wants. When I was in the war they used to call me 'Sleeper' instead of Seeper.'

He was an undersized man, with a thin face that was of a peculiar brick-red in colour, and thick hair that was almost jet black. The gas which had invalided him out of the army had left him with a permanent huskiness, and one of his most irritating qualities was that he would sing in a tuneless whisper while he went about his work.

At first this had almost driven Arnold to distraction, but after a little he had got used to it, for there was no means of checking Mr. Seeper of this habit.

'Blimey! What's the time, sir?' he asked as he peered about the semi-darkened room.

'It's half-past six,' said Arnold severely. 'What time did you go to bed?'

'I sat up till three waitin' for you,' answered Mr. Seeper, rubbing his face vigorously to try and disperse the hazy mists of sleep that still enshrouded his senses. ''Ave you only jest come 'ome, sir?'

'That's all,' said Arnold. 'We can't all lead lives of ease and luxury. Some of us have got to work. Let me have that coffee as soon as you can.'

He left Mr. Seeper to crawl reluctantly from his bed and going into the bathroom turned on the taps. He was feeling desperately tired. It was twenty-four hours since he had had any sleep at all, and the night had been a heavy one. From the moment the news had come into Scotland Yard concerning the burglaries he had scarcely had a second to think. Every available man had been pressed into service, and throughout the night the big building had been a hive of bustling industry.

The discoveries had been made almost simultaneously, and this was due to the fact that the thieves, although they had taken every precaution in effecting entrance to the various shops, had in every case left by the main door, the lock of which had been shattered. It was the various patrols going their rounds and trying these doors that had first given the alarm. In most cases the owners and managers of the shops lived above the premises, but so skilfully had the robberies been carried out that they had heard nothing, and their first intimation that anything had happened had been given by the policeman when he had discovered the door to be unfastened. The timing had been perfect, for the thieves had entered and made their get-away between the various policemen's rounds, and this argued an intimate knowledge of the police routine in the various districts.

'The whole thing was planned to the last detail,' said Chief Inspector Chedley, a harassed and worried man, 'and it looks to me as if we're up against the biggest thing in crime organisation that anyone's ever heard of.'

In none of the fourteen cases had, at the time Arnold left the Yard, a single clue been found. That it was the work of the same people who had successfully cleared the Western Bank was a foregone conclusion.

'And we haven't heard the last of them,' said Chedley, 'you mark my words. They're a smart crowd, and this is only the beginning.'

How right he was was proved in the weeks that followed.

Arnold thought over the events of the night as he lowered his shivering body into the cold bath he had drawn. Organised crime such as this did not belong to reality. It was the copyright of the sensational novelist, or had been up to now. Race-gangs and such like were common, but an organisation controlled by a master mind had been hitherto unknown. And yet there was no real reason why such a thing should not come into being, provided the man at the head of it was possessed of the necessary qualifications.

Arnold stepped out of the ice cold water and towelled himself briskly. His eyes were a little hot and smarted slightly but his intense weariness had left him. As he finished dressing the fragrant smell of coffee permeated the tiny flat, and when he entered the small living room George Seeper, looking a little more human, was just setting down the contents of a tray.

'Would you like some breakfast, sir?' he asked, and Arnold, who, before his bath, had not considered the possibility of food, nodded.

'I think it's a very good suggestion, George,' he answered.

'I'll 'ave it ready in a couple of jiffs,' said the servant, and as he poured out the coffee, 'What was up last night, sir?'

'All the balloons that were ever

invented!' said Arnold gravely, and seeing the astonishment on the other's face proceeded to enlighten him.

Mr. Seeper's thin lips pursed themselves into a shrill whistle.

'Blimey!' he ejaculated. 'Fourteen 'busts' in one night! That's goin' some. Who's at the bottom of it?'

'That's what I'd like to know,' said Arnold. 'So would several other people I'm acquainted with.'

'Must be a clever feller whoever he is,' said Mr. Seeper scratching his chin.

'And a newcomer,' remarked Arnold. 'None of the regulars 'd be capable of carrying through anything so big.'

'Well, it looks as if you've got a big job,' said Mr. Seeper. 'I wish yer luck!'

He went away to prepare the breakfast, shaking his head as though he had no hope that his wish would be fulfilled.

Arnold was free from duty until six o'clock that evening, and was looking forward with pleasurable anticipation to his appointment that afternoon with Penelope Hayes. He thought of this as he ate his leisurely breakfast. The excitement of the night had left him no time to think about the girl, but now that, for a space, his time was more or less his own, he found her again taking possession of his thoughts. She was another mystery. Almost as great a one as the identity of the people responsible for the successful series of robberies.

He would have given much to know why Deptford held such a fascination for her. Her story about visiting an old nurse was patently untrue. There was some other and more vital reason for her visit to the unsalubrious neighbourhood of Tanner's Hill. People do not go to the length of using chloroform in order to prevent a girl visiting her old nurse. There was something very strange about that episode, and Arnold was convinced that the girl was not as ignorant about it as she had pretended.

He was beginning to feel tired again, and was contemplating snatching a few hours' sleep when the postman's knock preceded the arrival of George with a letter.

'Jest come,' announced the servant unnecessarily.

Arnold took the dirty-looking envelope and frowned at the pencilled superscription. It was an ill-written scrawl and wondering who it could be from he slit open the envelope and withdrew the single sheet of paper it contained.

*'Dear Mr. Lake,'* he read. *'I think I know something. Could I see you tonight? I'll be at the bottom of Shardiloes Road at ten.Ernie Williams.'*

Arnold's face cleared as he came to the signature. He remembered now that he had once given the little 'nose' his address in case he should have anything of importance to communicate. Evidently Ernie had something of importance. Perhaps he had discovered something further about the unknown gang who were operating so successfully.

Arnold put the letter in his pocket, gave orders that he was to be called punctually at three, and going into his bedroom lay down on the bed and was asleep almost before he had finished pulling the eiderdown over him.

He slept soundly until he was awakened by Mr. Seeper with a cup of tea, and then washing and changing into another suit he left the flat to keep his appointment with Penelope Hayes at the Park Hotel.

He was a little early, but she was waiting for him in the vestibule, fresh and smiling and apparently none the worse for her adventure of the previous night. They went into the Palm Court and she eyed him critically as he ordered tea.

'You look tired,' she said. 'Were you up late?'

'I was up very early,' he answered. 'To be truthful it was nine o'clock this morning before I went to bed.'

She made a little grimace.

'They must work you very hard in the police force,' she remarked.

'It's not exactly the easiest of professions,' he admitted. 'You look very well.'

'I went to bed like a Christian,' she retorted. 'What was it kept you up all night?'

He told her, and she listened interestedly.

'That kind of thing is more prevalent in America than over here,' she said, and Arnold was quick to seize the opportunity.

'Do you know America well?' he asked.

She seemed absurdly confused at such an innocent question.

'Yes — I know it rather well,' she replied. 'I — I've lived there most of my life.'

He was surprised.

'But you're not an American?' he said.

She shook her head.

'No, I'm not American,' she answered, and steered the conversation quickly into other channels.

Arnold was puzzled and a little piqued. Why was this girl so secretive about herself? A dozen questions hovered on the tip of his tongue, but he remembered his promise of the night before and refrained from putting any of them.

Suddenly, as she was pouring out a second cup of tea she looked up.

'Have you ever heard of a man called Clark Quinton?' she asked.

The question, coming apropos of

nothing, rather surprised Arnold.

'No,' he replied. 'Who is he?'

'He's the worst man in the world!' she said vehemently. 'There is nothing so bad that Clark Quinton wouldn't do it.'

He stared at her in astonishment. The softness of her eyes had hardened and her lips were compressed.

'Is he a criminal?' he asked.

'A criminal that's never been caught,' she said bitterly. 'If you ever come across Clark Quinton be very careful, Mr. Lake.'

He was so taken aback that for the moment he could think of nothing to say.

'What do you know of this man?' he enquired at last.

'Nothing to his credit,' she said. 'I met him in America, but I believe he's now in England. That's why I asked you if you'd ever heard of him.'

He could see that she was sorry she had brought the subject up. She had put the question on the spur of the moment and instantly regretted it. Seeing this, he allowed the subject to drop, and for the remainder of his visit they talked about casual things.

Arnold found to his delight that the girl was interested in a number of things that interested him, and they chatted gaily, passing from topic to topic until, glancing at her watch, she uttered an exclamation of surprise.

'I'd no idea it was so late,' she said. 'Half-past five, and I've got an appointment at a quarter to six.'

She picked up her bag and passed a tiny puff over her face while he called the waiter and settled the bill.

'Will you see me into a taxi?' she said, and he escorted her through the vestibule.

On the way he extracted a promise from her to lunch with him on the following Friday.

'I don't know whether I ought to agree,' she said mischievously. 'Being seen about with a detective from Scotland Yard is not particularly good for one's reputation.'

They came down the steps of the hotel into the street and Arnold hailed a passing cab.

'Tell him to drive to Maison Linette,' she said in answer to his question as he assisted her into the waiting machine.

He closed the door, gave the order to the driver, and stood bareheaded as the taxi moved away from the sidewalk. As he was replacing his hat and turning away somebody tapped him on the shoulder, and looking round he encountered the smiling gaze of a tall, bony-faced man whose lean jaws moved rythmically.

'Hello, Nansen!' greeted Arnold as he shook the other's hand. 'What are you doing, sightseeing?'

Captain John E. Nansen, of the New York Detective Bureau, who was spending a holiday in England nodded slowly.

'I guess you're right, boy,' he drawled. 'Seein' sights is just what I'm doin'. Who was that dame you was puttin' in that cab?'

'A friend of mine,' said Arnold a little stiffly, rather resenting the other's tone.

'H'm!' The gaunt man shifted the gum he was chewing from one side of his mouth to the other. 'Well, she's a good looker, I'll say that. But I guess she's not the sort of friend a risin' police officer oughter keep company with.'

Arnold felt his colour rising.

'What do you mean?' he demanded. 'Miss Hayes is — '

'Hayes?' interrupted the American. 'Is that what she's callin' herself now.'

'It happens to be her name!' snapped Arnold shortly.

'It wasn't when I knew her over the other side,' said Captain Nansen shaking his head. 'She called herself Marion Hayford then.'

'You've made a mistake — ' began Arnold.

'No I haven't,' broke in the other. 'If there's any mistake it's yours! That was Marion Hayford right enough. One of the cleverest crooks who ever came up before a judge. And if she's in England you can bet the police here are goin' to have their hands full of trouble before very long!'

# 7

## Fay Langley

Considering that Mr. Ely Sholter had not reached his bed until after half-past eleven that morning he looked an exceedingly spruce and wakeful man as at six o'clock he left the vestibule of the block of flats in which he lived and got into the car which he had summoned by telephone. After leaving the unknown he had gone home, had a bath and changed, fortified himself with a good breakfast, and returned to the garage in Waterloo Road. At nine-thirty had come Weinderg, punctual to the minute, a little shabbily dressed hooked-nosed man, who spoke to the accompaniment of much gesticulation of his none too clean hands. For an hour they had argued and haggled over the heap of miscellaneous jewellery which had been carefully housed in the underground vault, the entrance to which was so carefully concealed.

This was one of the few alterations which Mr. Sholter had had done when he had taken over the garage from its previous owners. The vault was constructed of reinforced concrete faced with steel, and admission could only be gained by the eighteen inch thick door, and then only by such people who knew the combination which worked the intricate locks. And the only person who knew this was Mr. Sholter himself, and it was changed daily.

When the fence had grumblingly made his bargain and a large wad of notes had passed into the eager hands of Mr. Sholter the jewellery was transfered by that gentleman and the weary Billing from the vault to a special compartment under the seat of one of the Fleet Cabs. Into this Mr. Weinderg insinuated his dingy form and was driven off to his equally dingy office in an obscure street near Aldgate. The day manager took charge of the garage and Mr. Sholter went home to seek a much-needed rest.

As his comfortable car took him swiftly

towards Kensington he mentally rehearsed his forthcoming interview, and by the time the machine came to a halt in front of the imposing entrance to one of those new blocks of flats which are springing up everywhere he had settled on the way he would approach the business on which he was engaged.

Getting heavily out of the car, he told the chauffeur to wait, and entering the vestibule examined the indicator board screwed into one of the marble walls. The person he sought occupied a flat on the first floor, and the automatic lift deposited him within a short distance of the polished front door. Pressing an onyx button at the side of this resplendent portal Mr. Sholter waited. There was the sound of a soft footfall and the front door opened to reveal a trim maid who looked at him enquiringly.

Mr. Sholter produced a card and gave it to the girl.

'Will you take that to your mistress?' he said.

The maid glanced at the card, invited him into the hall, and closed the door softly behind him.

'Will you wait a moment, sir,' she said, and crossing to a door on the right tapped gently and disappeared within.

Mr. Sholter waited complacently, eyeing the appointments of the square lobby approvingly. In less than a minute the maid came back and intimated that her mistress would see him. Mr. Sholter deposited his hat on a settle and was ushered into a large room, prettily furnished as a lounge-drawing room.

The girl who sat curled up in a corner of the enormous settee was small and dainty. She had the fragile prettiness associated with Dresden china and her big blue eyes regarded Mr. Sholter with a half-timid, wholly-wondering expression, that quite a number of people found irresistible. The majority of these were of the male sex, for women had a disconcerting habit of seeing through Fay Langley's mask of baby innocence to the rather hard calculating nature it concealed, and were not impressed.

'Hello, Fay,' said Mr. Sholter genially. 'Every time I see you you look prettier!'

She gave an impatient twitch to one shoulder.

'Sit down, Sholter,' she said shortly, 'and cut out the compliments. What's brough you here?'

Mr. Sholter sank comfortably into a huge armchair.

'If I said it was the pleasure of seeing you again,' he murmured, 'I should be speaking the truth.'

'And that would be unusual,' said the girl, leaning forward and snipping open a silver box on a low table near her and helping herself to a cigarette.

Her real name was Chivvers, and the man who had bestowed it upon her was serving a life sentence in Dartmoor, and should have been hanged if the sentimental jury had not recommended him to mercy.

'You will have your little joke,' said Mr. Sholter. 'How are things, Fay?'

'Not too good,' she said, allowing a stream of smoke to trickle gently from between her red lips. 'There aren't so many mugs as there used to be, Sholter, and sex appeal doesn't pay a big dividend these days.'

Mr. Sholter glanced round the expensively-furnished room.

'You don't seem to be doing too badly,' he remarked.

She shrugged her shoulders.

'You wouldn't say that if you could take a peek in there.' She waved her cigarette towards a fragile-looking bureau that stood against one wall.

'Bills?' he asked sympathetically, and she nodded.

'Hundreds of 'em,' she said briefly. 'One of those drawers is chock full.'

He made a clucking sound with his tongue against the roof of his mouth.

'Dear, dear. I'm sorry to hear this, Fay,' he said. 'I always thought you were one of the lucky ones. Didn't you succeed in squeezing twenty thousand pounds out of young Lord Revelthorne? Somebody whispered to me that you did.'

'That was a year ago,' said Fay, 'and to a girl with my tastes twenty thousand doesn't go far.'

'It's a great pity, Fay,' said Mr. Sholter after a pause, 'that you can't marry a rich man.'

'It's a great pity,' retorted the girl sarcastically, 'but bigamy never was one of my hobbies, and Joe would take a lot of living down.' She swung her legs off the settee and eyed a slim, silk-clad ankle approvingly. 'I suppose you didn't come to see me because you were worried about my welfare?'

'Why not?' said Mr. Sholter. 'I've always been interested in you, Fay, you know that. In fact I've suggested more than once that when you get tired of the game and feel like security — '

'My idea of security is not becoming Mrs. Sholter,' she interrupted frankly. 'Apart from the fact that while Joe is alive my marrying again is impossible, you're the last man I should choose.'

Mr. Sholter shook his head sadly.

'Pity,' he said. 'We'd have made a good pair, Fay. You've got the looks and I've got the brains. Joe's certainly been a stumbling block to you. I wonder what some of these fellows you've rooked would have given to know that Joe existed?'

'Quite a lot, I imagine,' said Fay coolly. 'But I'm not proud of the fact that I'm married to a convict, and I don't advertise it.'

'Very sensible,' said Mr. Sholter. 'So things are not too good, eh, Fay?'

She looked at him suspiciously.

'What is all this leading to?' she asked.

He surveyed her steadily and rubbed his chin gently.

'Maybe I could put something in your way,' he said.

'I thought there was a business end to your visit,' said the girl. 'But it was always a habit of yours to go all round the map before you came to the point. Let's hear it.'

He leaned forward in his chair.

'What would you be prepared to do for five thousand pounds?' he asked.

'Anything, short of murder,' she retorted quickly. 'What's the proposition?'

'There's a girl living at the Park Hotel, Knightsbridge,' said Mr. Sholter slowly, 'who I'd like you to get acquainted with.'

'What's her name?' said Fay.

'Penelope Hayes,' he answered.

'Well, it shouldn't be difficult to get acquainted with her,' said the girl. 'What happens after that?'

'You might invite her round here to tea one day,' he suggested meaningly. 'Give your maid the afternoon off and get the tea yourself.' He dipped his hand into his waistcoat pocket and produced a little bottle. 'See that a couple of drops of this are put in her cup, and the five thousand is yours.'

'Oh, yes?' said the girl. 'And what happens when the kick comes? What happens when the girl lays information that she was drugged at my flat? No, thank you, Sholter! I've kept clear of trouble up to now, and I'm going to continue to keep clear.'

'There'll be no trouble,' he said, 'and no kick'll come. You needn't be afraid that the girl will make a fuss, because she won't. I and a friend of mine will be in the flat, and the moment she's asleep we'll take her away. So far as you're concerned that's the last you'll hear of her.'

'And the last anyone else'll hear of her, eh?' whispered Fay accusingly. 'I said I'd do anything short of murder, Sholter.'

'Who's talking about murder?' Mr. Sholter's sandy eyebrows rose in well-simulated surprise. 'Nothing's going to happen to the girl. As a matter of fact you'll be doing her a good turn.'

'It sounds like it,' interjected Fay.

'It's the truth,' said Mr. Sholter. 'I wouldn't deceive you, Fay. No harm'll come to that girl except a headache.'

'Well, she won't get the headache through me,' said Fay decisively. 'You try somebody else, Sholter. I'm not in on this. It sounds too risky to me.'

'Now don't be a silly girl,' he urged. 'Five thousand pounds is five thousand pounds, Fay, and apart from that there are several things you wouldn't like to become public property, I'm sure.'

His voice was smooth but his eyes were steely hard.

'I see,' she said. 'You're trying a little blackmail, eh?'

'That's a terrible thing to accuse an old friend of, Fay,' he protested. 'How can I blackmail you when I'm offering you five thousand pounds to do a little job? Would it be my fault if it became public property that you were married to a feller who was doin' a lifer on the 'Moor.' *I* wouldn't dream of telling anyone, but you know how these things leak out.'

'I know how they leak out when you're about,' she said, her lips curling. 'Well, when do you want this job done?'

He gave a sigh of relief. Her capitulation had been easier than he had anticipated.

'As soon as possible, Fay,' he said. 'This week, if you can manage it.'

'You're a nasty piece of work, Sholter,' she said dispassionately. 'I don't think there's anything so dirty but you wouldn't do it.'

'Oh, come, come, Fay,' he said. 'You don't mean that!'

'I do,' she retorted. 'But apparently I've got no choice but to do what you ask. You'll have to pay me half the money down, though.'

'You shall have it tomorrow, by the first post,' he promised.

'All right.' She nodded. 'Then I'll let you know when I've fixed the invitation.'

'That's a good girl,' he said, rising to

his feet. 'I thought you'd be sensible, Fay, you've got too many brains not to know which side your bread's buttered.'

He came over and patted her on the shoulder.

'Keep your filthy paws to yourself!' she said disgustedly. 'The five thousand pounds doesn't include your right to maul me about!'

Mr. Sholter's face was sorrowful as he turned away.

'You're getting temperamental, Fay,' he said. 'That's your trouble. Well, I'll expect to hear from you in a day or two.'

He took his departure, and as she heard the front door close softly behind him she uttered an 'Ugh!' of disgust, and going over to the window flung it wide.

Fay Langley was pretty hard-boiled, but there were some things she hated intensely, and Mr. Ely Sholter was one of them.

# 8

## A Dangerous Woman

Standing in the middle of the crowded pavement Arnold Lake stared dumbly at the American detective, unable to believe that he was serious.

'There must be some mistake,' he said, and was surprised to find that his voice was hoarse and unnatural.

Captain Nansen shook his head sympathetically.

'I guess there isn't,' he answered. 'I'd know that dame anywhere. Did you think she was the innocent baby? Well you're not the first guy she's caught with that stuff! Half the hard-boiled dicks in America thought the same until she was found out.'

Arnold swallowed with difficulty.

'Are you sure?' he persisted huskily. 'Perhaps it's only a chance resemblance.'

'Don't you kid yourself, son,' broke in

the American kindly. 'I don't make those kinda mistakes. There ain't so many good-lookers in the world as Marion Hayford, and anyone who's seen her once wouldn't be likely to forget her in a hurry, and I had my lamps on her every day for nearly a month.' He patted Arnold on the shoulder with a bony hand. 'I'm glad I happened to be around to put you wise,' he went on. 'She's a dangerous woman, and you can't breathe the same air as she does without getting in some kind of trouble. If you take my advice you'll give her a hundred yards' start and then run in the opposite direction.'

He took a packet of chewing gum from his waistcoat pocket, unwrapped the thin wafer and slipped it into his mouth. Arnold, who was still a little dazed by the startling revelation, pulled himself together.

'What did she do in America?' he asked in a more normal tone.

'What didn't she do!' said Captain Nansen. 'She was the fliest bird that ever came up against the Federal authorities. Peddling dangerous drugs was what she was convicted for.'

'Convicted!' broke in Arnold. 'Do you mean she's been in prison?'

The gaunt American nodded.

'Yes, sir,' he answered. 'In spite of the fact that an American jury is notoriously sentimental, they couldn't get round the evidence against her, and she was sentenced to five years. She'd be in prison now if she hadn't been lucky. She'd served two years of her sentence when a fire broke out in the Governor's quarters and she saved the life of his little daughter. The rest of her sentence was remitted for that. That was six or seven months ago. I suppose she thought she was too well known in America and hopped across to England believing she'd have more chance this side. The trouble is she's got a brain behind that pretty exterior. It takes a brain to be the head of the finest gang of dope runners that ever gave a police chief insomnia. For organisation that dame's got every big business man beaten to a frazzle.'

Arnold listened stunned. That there was something peculiar about Penelope Hayes he had known the first time he had met her in the charge-room at Meadow Lane police station. But that she was a convicted criminal had never entered his head. If the American detective was speaking the truth, and there was no reason to doubt his word, for he was a reliable man not given to making wild statements, it was no wonder that the girl had been reticent about her past. And yet, in spite of what he had just heard, the young inspector found it difficult to reconcile crime of any description with the smiling-faced girl whom he had a moment before assisted into a taxi.

It was true that he knew little about her, and experience had taught him that to judge a person from outward appearances was apt to lead to an erroneous conception of their character. One of the most charming men he had ever met had been convicted of a particularly brutal murder, and suffered the extreme penalty of the law. And he knew a man whose face would have hanged him whose hobby was child welfare, and who gave the greater part of his considerable income away to charity.

But with Penelope Hayes — he couldn't think of her as Marion Hayford — he would have vouched for her honesty. It seemed impossible that she could be capable of anything that was remotely approaching crookedness. He said as much to Nansen, and the big American smiled cynically.

'Would you be so ready to champion her if her eyes were squeeny and she had a complexion like muddy water? You wouldn't, boy, and you may as well admit it,' he said. 'You wouldn't think twice about believing what I've told you if her hair was coarse and strawly and she had a snub nose and thick ankles. Because she's a good looker and carries an expression as though butter wouldn't melt in her mouth, you'd give her a passport to Heaven!'

Arnold coloured, for he realised there was truth in what the other said.

'Well,' he said smiling wryly, 'you've certainly given me something to think about.'

He was shaking hands with the lean man when he remembered the question

Penelope had put to him at tea.

'Was there a fellow called Clark Quinton mixed up with the business?' he asked.

'You mean with Hayford?' asked Nansen, and when Arnold nodded: 'I can't recollect the name. Why?'

'I just wondered,' said the young inspector, and left him more than a little curious to know what had prompted that final question.

On his way to report at the Yard, Arnold found his recent talk with the American filling his thoughts to the exclusion of all else. Only now did he fully realise the extent of his interest in the girl. Obviously his wisest course, now that he had more or less accidentally discovered who she was, would be to have nothing more to do with her. But even while his conscious mind was dealing practically with the situation, his subconscious was whispering that there might be extenuating circumstances for her lapse into crime.

Over and over again during the journey from Knightsbridge to Westminster Arnold told himself that he was a fool. His continued association with Penelope could result in no good, and certainly if the truth concerning her came to light would be looked on askance by his superiors at Scotland Yard. Yet, although he told himself this, he knew he had no intention of acting on his own advice. The luncheon appointment he had made for the following Friday would be kept.

Reaching Scotland Yard he found a summons waiting for him, and made his way to the office of Superintendent Glinder, Chief of the Mobile Squad.

'Come in, Lake,' said the grey-haired man looking across his littered desk as Arnold entered the bare office. 'I want to talk to you about this sudden outbreak of crime.' He searched among the papers on his desk and finding the one he was looking for glanced at it rapidly. 'In this report of yours,' he went on, 'you mention that 'Cosh' Martin uttered some sort of threat against you and the police in general.'

'That's right,' assented Arnold. 'He did. As near as I can remember he hinted that there was a fellow coming who was going to cause us all a lot of trouble.'

Superintendent Glinder nodded.

'That's what I'm talking about,' he said. 'Now, there's no doubt, unusual as it may be, that these crimes are being very carefully organised by one person. In other words the master criminal which we've always smiled about in fiction has put in an appearance in real life. And I'm wondering whether 'Cosh' knew something and was referring to this man.'

'I've thought the same, sir,' said the young inspector.

'Well, I want you to go to Pentonville tomorrow and see if you can get anything out of this fellow Martin,' said the Superintendent. 'I'll arrange a permit for you to see him in the morning. I don't know that it'll do much good, but we've got to try everything. Try and find out what he meant when he mentioned this man.'

'Has anything further come to light, sir, about the robberies?' asked Arnold.

The Chief of the Mobile Squad shook his head.

'No, nothing,' he answered briefly. 'And

I'm doubtful if anything will. We're not dealing with the ordinary type of criminal; we're dealing with a genius at organisation. It's my opinion that it's our department that'll eventually run these people to earth.'

Although Arnold was unaware of the fact he was merely passing on a remark made by the Assistant Commissioner on the previous evening.

'These people have got to move quickly, and when we discover how they move it will be up to the Squad. Keep a look out for any suspicious-looking cars or vehicles of any kind during your patrol, and don't hesitate to pull in any one who can't satisfy you as to their bona fides. In future every car will carry a full crew in case of emergency.'

This was a little disconcerting. Unless Arnold turned up alone to keep his appointment with Ernie Williams that suspicious man would remain dumb. He explained this to the Superintendent, and the grey-haired man rubbed his chin thoughtfully.

'H'm, well, you'd better use your own

discretion,' he said presently. 'In any particular case like that you can waive the order, but ordinarily no 'Q' car is to carry less than three men besides the driver and the wireless operator.'

It was seven o'clock when Arnold left the Yard and drove slowly towards Deptford. He was doubtful if his interview with 'Cosh' Martin would lead to anything. He had questioned the little crook pretty thoroughly in Meadow Lane police station on the night he had snarled his warning, without result. That the man did know something he was pretty sure, but whether he could be persuaded to divulge what he knew was another matter. He had shut up like an oyster in the charge-room, but that was possibly because he was afraid of the consequences. Safe at Pentonville he might be less reticent.

Arnold came slowly along the narrow confines of Meadow Lane and pulled up outside the station house. Sergeant Fisk was laboriously writing in his book when he entered the charge-room and looked over his glasses with a smile.

'Evening, sir,' he greeted. 'You seem to have been having a lot of excitement at the Yard. I've just been readin' the papers, fourteen burglaries in one night. Somebody's been busy.' He shook his head. 'What with them and that bank business it looks as if we was in for a crime wave. Did you see that girl, Miss What's-her-name, home all right, sir?'

Arnold replied rather shortly. He had no wish to discuss Penelope Hayes, the revelation of Captain Nansen was still too fresh in his mind. But the desk-sergeant was a slow-thinking man and not easily put off a subject that he had once started on.

'I've been wonderin' a lot about her,' he went on. 'It seems funny to me that a lady like that should find any business to bring her to Deptford, don't you think so, sir?'

'Her explanation was that she was on her way to visit an old nurse,' said Arnold.

'Is that what she said?' Sergeant Fisk raised his eyebrows. 'Well, now, that's a bit curious, 'cause that time when she 'ad 'er bag snatched wasn't the first time she'd been in this district.'

'Oh. How do you know that?' said Arnold quickly.

'Well, I was talkin' to one of our men this mornin' about her,' answered the sergeant, 'and he remembered her comin' up to him and askin' the way to Viddle Street.'

'When was this?' said Arnold.

'About a week before the bag snatchin' business,' answered the sergeant.

Arnold frowned. The girl had distinctly said that the old nurse she was supposed to have been visiting lived on Tanner's Hill, so what had been her object in enquiring the way to Viddle Street?

'Perhaps it wasn't Miss Hayes,' he suggested, but the desk-sergeant was positive.

'I'm sure it was,' he affirmed. 'Denny's a pretty smart man, and he described her perfectly. Even down to that funny ring on her second finger. You know the one I mean, sir? A kind of a hess in green stones.'

Arnold did know the one he meant. He had noticed it the first time he had seen the girl, and thought what a curious design it was; an 'S' in emeralds set with two diamonds, one in each loop.

'Viddle Street's a funny sort of place for a girl like that to want to go to,' continued the sergeant. 'And that's why I can't help thinkin' it's peculiar.'

Viddle Street was one of the worst slums in Deptford, a narrow thoroughfare, indescribably dirty. By day and up till quite late at night the refuse-strewn gutters were usually full of shrieking children, wizened, half-starved mites, whose pinched faces were already beginning to acquire the shifty, furtive look that marked their parents. It was not to be wondered at that Sergeant Fisk had been surprised that a girl of Penelope's smartness should enquire the way to such an unsalubrious district.

Arnold sighed unconsciously and the sergeant looked at him sympathetically.

'Feelin' a bit tired, sir?' he said. 'I expect you had a heavy night.'

Arnold allowed him to think that weariness was the cause of that sigh, and the subject of Penelope Hayes and her strange behaviour was dropped.

When he left the station house and got into his car to keep his appointment with Ernie Williams he had come to a decision concerning the girl. During that luncheon which he had arranged for Friday he would tackle her with being Marion Hayford, and until then would try to put all thought of her out of his mind.

He reached the meeting place in Shardiloes Road just as the clock was striking ten, but there was no sign of little Ernie Williams. Bringing his car to a halt by the sidewalk he lit a cigarette and waited. Five minutes passed, and still the little 'nose' had not put in an appearance. Arnold began to wonder if something had happened to detain him. Shardiloes Road was deserted and although he leaned out of the open window and peered up and down he could see no sign of anyone approaching.

He decided to wait until a quarter past ten and then give it up. He had barely settled back in his seat when a cyclist turned in at the lower end of the road and began to ride slowly towards him. The flickering flame of his oil lamp drew nearer, and Arnold glanced sideways at him as the man passed close to the car on the off side. As he did so something fell into his lap, and looking down he saw by the light from the dashboard that it was an egg-shaped thing of metal — a Mills bomb, and the pin was out!

He had only a second to decide on his course of action, but it was enough. Seizing the bomb he thrust his arm through the window and threw it with all his force as far as he could. It fell in the middle of the roadway, and even as it struck there was a blinding flash and a shattering explosion, followed by the crash of breaking glass.

A little shakily Arnold got out of the car. He had been nearer to death in the last sixty seconds than he ever wished to be again during the rest of his life!

# 9

## What Ernie Knew

The echoes of the explosion had barely died away when the deserted street became miraculously filled with an excited crowd of chattering people. Arnold looked round for the cyclist, but he had disappeared. No doubt after dropping that little globe of death through the car window he had pedalled away for dear life.

Arnold found himself surrounded by a curious crowd, comprised mostly of the inhabitants of Shardiloes Road, who had hastily left their houses to discover the cause of this disturbance of their peace. He was bombarded with questions, and then to his relief he heard the shrill blast of a police whistle, and saw the helmet of a constable appear at the back of the throng.

''Ere, what's all this?' the man demanded

as he forced his way to Arnold's side. 'Was it your car that made that noise?'

'No, it wasn't,' said Arnold, and in a low voice rapidly explained who he was, and what had happened.

The amazed constable scratched his chin.

'A bomb!' he said incredulously. 'I thought it was your car what had blown up.'

'It nearly was,' said Arnold grimly. 'Let's go and see what damage has been done to the road.'

He began to elbow his way through the gaping crowd, and presently came to the spot where the bomb had struck. A ragged hole had been torn in the centre of the road nearly six feet in diameter. Luckily it had missed any main water or gas pipes there may have been, but the force of the explosion had shattered every pane of glass in the windows of the houses in the immediate vicinity.

Reinforcements of police came running up, and when the situation had been explained they took charge of the crowd and began to send them back to their homes. The fact that the explosion had been caused by a bomb had leaked out, and the vague scraps of excited comments reached Arnold's ears as the residents of the street were shepherded back to their houses.

'Can you describe this man on the bicycle, sir?' enquired a sergeant who had arrived while the police were dealing with the throng.

Arnold shook his head.

'No,' he answered. 'Except that he was dressed in a dark suit. I never saw his face at all. He had a cap pulled low over his eyes and a muffler which covered his mouth.'

One of the policemen came back at that moment and gave him a dirty scrap of paper.

'A man gave me this, sir,' he said, 'and asked me to give it to you.'

Arnold looked at the writing and saw that it was from Ernie Williams. In the light of one of the 'Q' car's lamps he read the ill-written message:

'*I saw what happened. I'll be waiting for you at eleven at the end of Kitto Road and Drakefell Road. E.W.*'

He crumpled the paper and thrust it into his pocket. The reason for this attempt on his life puzzled him, until it suddenly occurred to him that it might have been to prevent his meeting with the little 'nose.' Had these people become aware that Ernie Williams had information to offer? If so, why hadn't they gone after *him?* It would have been easier and less dangerous to have tackled Williams. Perhaps the man on the bicycle had been under the impression that Williams was already in the car, and his intention had been to kill two birds with one stone. That seemed plausible. One thing was certain. Whatever reason lay behind the attempt, it had been a very narrow escape. If the bomb had not fallen into his lap, if it had fallen on to the floor of the car, he would never have seen what it was, and by the time he had groped about and found it, it would have been all over.

The Divisional Inspector had been sent for, and by the time he arrived and Arnold had given him the facts of the matter it was nearing eleven. Leaving the inspector and the sergeant to deal with the routine enquiries and superintend the erection of a barricade round the crater in the roadway, he re-entered the 'Q' car and drove slowly off towards the juncture of Drakefell and Kitto Roads. As he slowed at the corner a figure darted from the shadows of a gateway and sprang on to the running board.

'Don't stop, Mr. Lake,' whispered a hoarse voice, and as Arnold obeyed Ernie Williams dexterously opened the door and slid into the seat by his side.

'So you saw the fireworks, did you?' said Arnold. 'What did you think of the display?'

The little 'nose' was breathless, and it was some seconds before he could answer.

'I was scared stiff,' he confessed. 'I turned into the road as the thing went off. What happened?'

Arnold told him.

'What a bit of luck you managed to throw it away,' said Ernie Williams with a shiver. 'I tell you, Mr. Lake, you're up against a tough crowd. From what I can hear this bunch'll stick at nothin'.'

'What did you have to tell me?' asked Arnold.

His companion licked his lips nervously.

'You remember my tellin' yer that it was my idea some Big Feller was tryin' to form a gang?' he said.

Arnold nodded.

'Yes, and from what's happened since I believe you were right,' he answered.

'I know I'm right, Mr. Lake,' said the little man. 'It's the talk of the district that there's a Big Boss with big ideas, and all the little crooks are tumblin' over each other in their eagerness to get in with 'im. They don't speak about it openly, but if yer keeps yer ears skinned you can get a word 'ere and there. Somebody's runnin' things on a big scale and payin' big money.'

'Who?' demanded Arnold.

Ernie shook his head.

'I don' know that,' he answered, 'and I don't think any of the others knows either. They gets their orders from various fellers and they don' know themselves who the Big Noise is. There's an 'eadquarters somewhere where the stolen stuff's taken to. I've found out that much, but I don' know where it is.'

'You don't seem to know very much about anything,' said Arnold a little irritably.

The few hours' sleep he had had and the shock of his recent narrow escape had affected his temper.

'I 'opes to know quite a lot soon,' said the little 'nose,' 'but I thought you'd like to know that that gang I told you about before really existed. There ain't no doubt about that.'

'Is that all you wanted to see me for?' demanded Arnold. 'We knew there was a gang in existence. We didn't want you to tell us.'

Mr. William's thin voice assumed an injured whine.

'I thought you'd like to know fer certain like,' he said plaintively. 'You've got to remember, Mr. Lake, that I can't do miracles. I'm doin' the best I can, an' I've got to be careful, too. If any of these fellers thought I was snoutin' on 'em they'd put me out as soon as drink a cup o' tea. You know that as well as I do.'

Arnold felt a little ashamed of his bad temper.

'All right, Ernie,' he said kindly. 'Don't take any notice of me. I'm a little bit rattled today.'

'I ain't surprised,' said the little 'nose.' 'Blimey! If I'd 'ad a bomb slung at me I'd 'ave been rattled, too!'

He sniffed, an unpleasant habit that was a sure sign he was excited.

'I wonder why they went after you?' he continued.

Arnold hesitated. He was pretty sure it was because of his appointment with the man beside him, but he had no wish to frighten him. On the other hand, if it was known that he had been going to meet Ernie Williams the little 'nose' ought to be warned in case, having failed to get Arnold with the bomb, they turned their attention to him.

He mentioned his suspicion.

'I don't see how anyone could 'ave known you was goin' to meet me,' said Ernie, but his voice was a little tremulous. 'Nobody could 'ave seen me write the

114

letter. I wrote it in me own room and posted it in a pillar box. You didn't tell no one you'd got it, did yer?' he added anxiously.

Arnold shook his head.

'Only Superintendent Glinder,' he replied.

'Then nobody could 'ave known I was meetin' yer,' said Ernie, and his tone was relieved. 'They must 'ave been followin' you. Per'aps they thought you was gettin' on to somethin'.'

This suggestion did not strike Arnold as very likely. There was no reason why he should be singled out more than anyone else at Scotland Yard. Less, in fact, for there were others in that grim building who were taking more active steps to check the new menace. It was all very mysterious, and yet someone had wanted to put him out of the running. Someone who had known that he would be at the bottom of Shardiloes Road at ten that night. Now how had they become possessed of this information? It was impossible that anyone could have seen the note written to him by Ernie Williams . . .

A sudden idea occurred to him. There was one person who could have seen that note. His servant, George Seeper! Arnold remembered Seeper's record. Was this how the information had leaked out? He couldn't bring himself to believe it. The little man had completely turned over a new leaf, and during the time he had been with him had served Arnold faithfully. It was unlikely that he would have made himself party to a plot on his master's life.

All the same, the doubt was there. George would have had plenty of opportunity to read that scrawled note while Arnold had been asleep. He remembered that after reading it he had thrust it into the pocket of his jacket, and when he had lain down he had taken that jacket off and hung it over a chair. His sleep had been so sound that Seeper could quite easily have crept into the room and read the message without his being any the wiser. Was that what had happened?

He made no mention of his suspicion to the little 'nose,' but mentally decided to take precautions in the future, and to

116

watch the sleepy George a little more closely than he had done before. It was an unpleasant thought that his own servant might be acting against him, and probably an unjust one, but it was just as well to take precautions.

He had been driving slowly through a maze of side streets and now came out into the Broadway.

'Where shall I drop you?' he asked.

'Anywhere where there ain't any people about,' answered Ernie. 'I'll telephone yer next time, Mr. Lake, when I've got any definite news. P'raps that'd be safer than writin'.'

'Telephone me to the Yard,' said Arnold, 'and leave a message with Superintendent Glinder if I'm not there. What you want to concentrate on, Ernie, is the fellow who's running this outfit. Never mind the smaller fry, they don't count. If we can once get hold of the big boss the others'll scatter like leaves before a high wind.'

'I'll do me best,' said Ernie, and as Arnold brought the car to a stop in a deserted side street he opened the door.

For a moment he hesitated before getting out.

'I wasn't goin' to tell yer,' he said, with one foot on the running board, 'because it's only a rumour I've 'eard an' I don't want ter put you wrong.'

'What is the rumour?' asked Arnold as he paused.

The little 'nose' seemed rather reluctant to tell him, and then apparently made up his mind.

'You was talkin' about the man who was at the 'ead of this bunch,' he said. 'Well, I've 'eard a rumour that it ain't a man, but a woman!'

He was gone before Arnold had recovered from the astonishment his words had inspired.

# 10

## The Man Who Lived in Viddle Street

Long after the last of the dirty little rag-a-muffins who used Viddle Street as a playground had gone to the pile of rags that for the most part constituted their beds, a slinking figure came furtively down the narrow, ill-lighted slum, keeping in the shadows and entered number ten, closing the door softly behind him, and the two men who were watching from the mouth of an alley on the opposite side of the road heard the rattle of a chain as the door was secured.

'That's 'im,' muttered the taller of the watchers, and his companion nodded.

The man who lived at number ten, unaware of their presence, passed silently along the dark and narrow passage and went into the kitchen. Striking a match he cautiously examined the fastening of the shutter that covered the window. Then he went into the tiny scullery and shot the bolt on the outer door. Having assured himself that it was shot, he lit a candle, and went slowly up the stairs. Reaching the landing he entered a room in the front of the house, set down the candle and taking off his coat flung it on the bed.

The room was stuffy and smelt of stale tobacco smoke, but he made no attempt to open the window.

He was a peculiar looking man, big-built and beetle-browed. The inhabitants of Viddle Street had speculated much concerning him when, three months previously, he had moved in to the empty number ten. He was apparently unmarried, for no woman had been seen about the house, and he kept himself very much to himself. So far as Viddle Street was concerned this was a point in his favour, for nearly the whole of the inhabitants are criminals of one sort or another, and are therefore very reticent about their own doings, and prefer this same reticence on the part of their neighbours.

Mr. Barney Gore was a night bird who kept to his house in the daytime, and only went out when respectable people were in bed and asleep.

Going to a cupboard he brought a pad of paper and a bottle of ink over to the table and searching for a pen he sat down and began to write. After three lines he paused and listened, and then, as though the fancied sound had suggested the omission he pulled a long-barrelled automatic from his pocket and laid it on the table beside him. Having taken this precaution he went on with his task, but not for long. The sound he had heard before came again.

Stealing softly to the door he opened it and bent his head. The noise he had heard came from the next house, for the walls were thin, and reassured he relocked the door and went back to the table.

He had covered a sheet with writing when again he stopped, and this time he knew he was not mistaken. Somebody was outside the house in the street below. He heard them at the front door.

Blowing out the candle which flickered on the table at his elbow he put the room in darkness. The floor creaked a little as he stepped over to the window and drew aside the torn and dusty blind. Raising the sash noiselessly he peeped out. In the dim light of a distant street lamp he saw two figures standing below. One was tapping the downstairs window.

Mr. Barney Gore slipped a flashlight from his pocket and suddenly a white beam of light struck down to the narrow street.

'Want anythin'?' he demanded in a harsh, uneducated voice. 'If you do, spit it out!'

The men below dropped their heads to hide their faces and the taller said:

'Come down, we want to speak to you.'

'Want ter speak to me do yer, what is it about?' demanded Mr. Gore.

'We can't tell you up there,' said the man who had spoken before. 'Come down.'

Gore hesitated. He knew very well what they wanted him for. Knew the risk he would take if he did go down. And then while he hesitated a burly form loomed up out of the shadows and at the approach of the uniformed figure the two men turned and walked quickly away. The man at the window muttered something below his breath.

'What's the matter?' called the constable. 'Any trouble?'

'No, no trouble,' said Gore surlily. 'Jest speakin' to two friends o' mine.'

The policeman moved on and Gore switched off his torch and closed the window. He re-lit the candle and sat down at the table with a frown of annoyance. But he did not resume his writing.

For nearly two hours he sat staring before him, apparently lost in thought, and then rising abruptly he slipped the automatic pistol into his pocket and pulled on his coat. Putting out the light he locked the door of his room behind him and made his way silently down the dark stairs. He made no sound as he eased back the bolt on the front door, and twisting the catch let himself out into the now deserted street.

Slinking along by the houses in much the same way as he had come, he shuffled rapidly along towards the main road, and behind him followed two shadowy figures as furtive as he himself. If he was aware of their presence he gave no sign, but continued on his way until he reached a narrow opening between two tall buildings and into this he turned. It led through to another street that ran parallel with Viddle Street, but Barney Gore only went two yards along it.

Stopping he swung round and crouched in the shadows — waiting.

The sound of stealthy steps came to his ears and drawing forth his pistol he thumbed back the safety-catch, and with the other hand took out his torch. The approaching steps stopped.

'He went down here,' a voice whispered huskily. 'Come on — we'll get him before he reaches the end. He couldn't have chosen a better spot.'

Two shapeless blobs obscured the entrance to the passage and turned in, and the man who crouched by the wall waited patiently, his lips set.

The two men who had been following him were within touching distance when he rose upright.

'Don't move or I'll shoot!' he rasped. 'I want ter see yer blinking faces!'

As the lamp in his hand flashed out the strangers ducked, and the nearest man, with a sudden kick, sent the torch flying from Gore's hand.

'Get him!' he hissed viciously, and sprang forward.

The automatic cracked, but the bullet went wide, and before Gore could fire again they were both on him. He clubbed the pistol and struck out, and one of his assailants gave a grunt of pain.

'Use the knife!' he snarled, and Gore saw a flicker of steel in the other's hand.

He lashed out with his left and caught the man on the point of the jaw, and then there came the thudding of rapidly-approaching feet and the shrill blast of a police whistle.

'Look out!' warned the man who had suggested the knife. 'Here come the flatties. Come on — clear!'

They took to their heels racing swiftly down the narrow passage and the man they had attacked rose to his feet. Thrusting his pistol into his pocket he, too, fled in the same direction, just as the bulky figure of a policeman peered into the mouth of the alley.

It seemed that Mr. Barney Gore was as much scared of the police as had been the men who tried to kill him.

# 11

## 'Cosh' Martin Refuses to Come Across

Arnold awoke from an uneasy sleep on the following morning to find a yawning George Seeper standing by his bedside with a cup of tea. A vague feeling of trouble for which he could not account possessed him as he struggled to a sitting posture and took the cup from his servant's hand.

'There's no letters,' said Mr. Seeper. 'When would you like your breakfast?'

Arnold sipped the scalding tea and blinked at him.

'What's the time?' he demanded huskily.

'Just gone seven,' answered George. 'I wouldn't be awake if they hadn't made a row next door goin' out.'

'Let's hope they do so every morning,' grunted Arnold. 'Perhaps we shall be able to keep respectable hours then. Run my bath and I'll have breakfast in half an hour.'

Mr. Seeper departed grumbling about 'inconsiderate neighbours,' and as the hot tea dispersed the last remnants of sleep from his brain Arnold succeeded in placing the reason for the troubled uneasiness which he had experienced at the moment of waking. It was due to Ernie Williams' remark just before he had left him on the previous night. The man's words had given rise to an almost incredible suspicion.

Penelope Hayes, according to Captain Nansen, had been at the head of a big dope syndicate in America. The American had remarked on her genius for organisation. Was it possible that she was behind the sudden outbreak of crime, or was the rumour the little 'nose' had mentioned only a rumour and nothing more? If the girl was mixed up in it, it would certainly explain her mysterious visits to Deptford, for it was from that district that the first report had reached Scotland Yard concerning the unrest among the criminal classes.

Arnold yawned, stretched himself, and getting out of bed slipped on a dressing gown. Rumours, rumours! he thought irritably, nothing but rumours. Looked at in the cold light of reason it seemed ridiculous to associate a girl like Penelope Hayes with the robbery of the Westland Bank. And yet the actual plan had been a simple one and could just as easily have been thought of by a woman as by a man.

He made his way along to the bathroom, shaved and had his bath, hoping that these normal proceedings would shake off the depression that overwhelmed him. But by the time he had dressed it was no better.

He was in something of a quandary, and while he ate the breakfast which George Seeper put before him, he tried to solve his difficulty. His duty was to acquaint his superiors at the Yard with all that he had learned. He knew that, but he could not make up his mind to do it. If he told Superintendent Glinder what Nansen had revealed on the previous night and added Ernie Williams' rumour, nothing was more certain than that enquiries would be set afoot immediately. Men would be detailed to probe into the girl's past, and her movements would be subjected to a constant watch. Throughout his meal Arnold wrestled with his problem, duty against personal inclination, and personal inclination won. Until he had seen the girl on the Friday he would do nothing.

During the days that followed he was to blame himself severely for this decision. For it was destined that that luncheon appointment was never to be kept and many things were to happen before he saw Penelope Hayes again.

The bomb outrage in Shardiloes Road had crept into the papers. He found, to his annoyance, half a column of it in the *Megaphone*, and the sight of it served to remind him of his suspicion concerning George Seeper. He smiled a little grimly as he pushed the paper away from him. He was full of suspicions these days; everybody he came in contact with seemed to be suspicious.

The little man came in answer to his ring and looked at him enquiringly.

'What d'you want?' he asked. 'More coffee?'

Arnold shook his head.

'No, I want a word with you, George,' he said.

'If it's about them eggs,' said the servant, 'I couldn't help it. If there'd been any more in the 'ouse I'd 'ave done 'em again.'

'It's got nothing to do with the eggs,' said Arnold impatiently. 'What was wrong with them anyway?'

'One of 'em was broke,' explained George. 'It broke as I was turnin' it. It's a tricky business fryin' them things.'

'I dare say it is,' interrupted his master, 'but I'm not interested in them at the moment. In fact but for a piece of luck I might never have been interested in them again, fried or otherwise.'

He handed the surprised George the paper and pointed to the column.

'Read that,' he said curtly.

Mr. Seeper obeyed and his small eyes were round as he took in its meaning.

'Blimey!' he ejaculated. 'You must have upset somebody pretty badly for 'em to try tricks like that.'

Arnold was watching him keenly, and if his amazement was not genuine he was a very good actor indeed.

'You knew nothing about it?' he said, and Mr. Seeper shook his head.

'Me?' he answered. 'No, 'ow should I know anything about it? I took the opportunity, as you was out, to go to bed early, and I didn't wake up until them infernal people began banging about next door. Sometimes I do 'ave a look at the paper while you're dressin', but you was in such an 'urry for your breakfast this mornin' that there weren't no time.' He put the newspaper down on the table and frowned. 'I don't like this,' he said. 'Bombs ain't English. There's a nasty, foreign touch about 'em. You go an' be careful or you'll be gettin' into trouble.'

There was concern in his voice, and Arnold was convinced that it was not put on. The little man was genuinely worried, and his half-formed suspicion against him evaporated. How the fact that he was going to be in Shardiloes Road at ten o'clock on the previous night had reached the ears of the person responsible for the bomb outrage he had no idea, but he was prepared to swear that George Seeper had no hand in it.

He dismissed the man, poured himself out a second cup of coffee and when he had swallowed it prepared to make his way down to the Yard.

Superintendent Glinder was in his office, and when Arnold came in produced a slip of paper and handed it to him.

'There's your permit to see 'Cosh' Martin,' he said. 'Go along and see him now. Do what you can to make him talk. What happened last night ought to be an added incentive for you to run these people to earth.'

Arnold set out for the Pentonville Road and reached the ugly prison building as the clocks were striking ten. He was admitted and conducted to the Governor's office. That gentleman examined his permit and sent for the Chief Warder.

'Inspector Lake has an order to interview number sixty-three,' he said. 'Take him along to his cell, will you.'

Arnold was conducted along a maze of stone corridors lined with steel doors and in front of one of these the warder stopped. Calling to the guard who was in charge of that particular section he ordered him to unlock the door, and the young inspector was shown into the presence of 'Cosh' Martin.

The little pickpocket was seated on his pallet bed, for the exercise hour was just over. He looked up with a scowl as Arnold came in, which changed to surprise when he saw who his visitor was.

'Hello, what d'you want?' he growled ungraciously. 'Come to gloat over yer work, 'ave you? Can't you busies leave a chap in peace?'

'I want to have a little talk to you, Martin,' said Arnold.

The prisoner grunted.

'Feelin' lonely or somethin'?' he asked sarcastically. 'Can't you go and talk to your blasted friends at Scotland Yard? Why come and bother me?'

'I'll be outside if you want me, sir,' said the warder, for the permit had authorised that Arnold was to hold his interview in private. 'You behave yourself now, Martin, and tell this gentleman what he wants to know.'

He went out, closing the door behind him and 'Cosh' Martin sneered.

'Gentleman?' he echoed. 'Since when have the police entered the aristocracy?'

'Since we began to take university men into the force,' answered Arnold good humouredly. 'Have a cigarette, Martin.'

He produced his case and Mr. Martin took one eagerly, but without relaxing his defensive attitude.

'You're bein' very friendly, ain't you?' he asked suspiciously.

'The police are always friendly,' answered Arnold, 'if you fellows would only realise it. We don't want to get you into trouble.'

'Of course you don't,' said 'Cosh' Martin sarcastically. 'That's why I'm 'ere. That rozzer who pinched me on Tanner's 'Ill was bein' friendly I suppose.'

'He was only doing his duty,' said Arnold. 'You know that, Martin.'

'Cosh' Martin drew in a mouthful of smoke and expelled it with a sigh of satisfaction.

'That's good,' he remarked. 'I suppose you 'aven't come 'ere to chat about the friendliness of the police, 'ave yer?'

Arnold shook his head.

'No, I've come to ask you one or two questions,' he said.

'I thought you was after somethin',' asserted Mr. Martin. 'When a busy starts givin' things away and becomes 'uman there's always a catch in it. What d'you want to know?'

'I want to know,' said Arnold, 'what you meant in Meadow Lane charge room when you hinted that there was some fellow or other coming who'd give us a lot of trouble.'

The expression of 'Cosh' Martin's face changed, his eyes narrowed and he examined the cigarette between his fingers.

'I didn't mean nothin',' he muttered.

'Oh, yes you did,' said Arnold. 'You meant just what you said. Come across now, Martin. It won't do you any harm.'

'It won't do me any good,' grunted the other. 'Squeakin' never did anyone any good. Besides, I don't know nothin'.'

'You mean you just made it up?' said Arnold, and Mr. Martin seized the suggestion quickly.

'That's right,' he replied. 'I just said it to annoy you.'

'You should become a prophet when you leave here,' said Arnold. 'Prophecy is evidently your strong suit.'

'What d'you mean?' growled 'Cosh.' 'Speak English, can't yer.'

'I mean you were a remarkably good guesser,' said Arnold. 'For the fellow you warned me against has turned up after all.'

'Must have been a coincidence,' said the other.

'Tell me something else,' retorted Arnold. 'Now, come, Martin. You knew very well what you were talking about. Spill it. You've got nothing to fear, you're safe enough here. Nobody can get back on you for your information.'

'Couldn't they,' said 'Cosh' Martin. 'The feller I was talkin' about'd get at yer if you was in 'ell. Not that there's much difference — '

He stopped abruptly.

'So there was a fellow, and you were talking about him,' said Arnold gently.

'Well, yes,' admitted the other sullenly. 'But I ain't talkin' about 'im any more, so you can save your breath.'

Arnold checked the impatient retort that rose to his lips. 'Cosh' Martin and men of his type could be very exasperating at times. But his training stood him in good stead, for patience is one of the assets of the Metropolitan Police Force.

'Why not be sensible?' he urged. 'I told you before you won't lose by it.'

'What you goin' to do,' said Mr. Martin, 'present me with a free pardon? You do that and I'll talk so much you'll 'ave to shove a gag in me mouth to stop me!'

'You know that's impossible,' said Arnold. 'But there'll be a good mark put against your name in records, and if you ever get into trouble again it'll go in your favour.'

'Get into trouble again,' said 'Cosh' Martin derisively. 'I ain't got out of this little lot yet.'

Arnold had an inspiration.

'You weren't working on your own when you snatched the girl's bag were you?' he asked. 'Didn't you say some fellow paid you to do the job?'

'Didn't I say,' repeated Mr. Martin scornfully. 'Why I ain't said nothin' else since I was pinched. I told that old so-and-so on the bench, and I told the prosecutin' counsel, but no one'd believe me. That fat feller offered me ten quid to pinch the bag and I took it on.'

'And was it he who told you about this other fellow?' said Arnold.

'Well, yes, it was,' grunted 'Cosh' Martin after a pause. 'But that wasn't the first I'd 'eard about 'im. Most of the chaps I knew round Deptford 'ad 'eard there was a Big Feller comin' who was out to clean up a packet. This feller I met in the pub seemed to know more about it than they did.'

'Oh, he did, eh?' said Arnold interestedly. 'Go on.'

But 'Cosh' Martin thought he had said enough.

'It ain't no good, Lake,' he declared frankly. 'I'm not talkin', and all the busies at the Yard can't make me.'

'You're being the strong, silent man, eh?' said Arnold sighing wearily.

'I don't know nothin' about no strong silent men,' retorted 'Cosh.' 'But if it means I'm sayin' nothin' you've hit it!'

Arnold stayed for another half hour, threatening, cajoling and almost pleading, but to no purpose. 'Cosh' Martin was adamant. Whether he knew anything or not was open to conjecture, but if he did he wasn't going to divulge it.

Arnold left the prison tired and a little sick at heart. He had hoped that his interview would do something to allay the doubt he had concerning Penelope Hayes, but although he had hinted to the pickpocket that it might be a woman and not a man whom he had meant Mr. Martin had refused to be drawn.

He reported his failure to Superintendent Glinder and that experienced man merely shrugged his shoulders.

'I wasn't too hopeful,' he confessed, 'but I thought something might have come of it. These fellows are as obstinate as mules, and just about as brainless.

Perhaps we can find this fat man he talked about. He told the detective at the court that he had sandy hair and a little moustache, so we've got something to go on.'

It was very little, had he but known it, for the sandy wig and moustache which Mr. Ely Sholter had worn on the occasion when he had interviewed 'Cosh' Martin had been destroyed immediately that enterprising gentleman had received the news of his employee's arrest.

# 12

## Mr. Sholter Strikes a Good Thing

With one of his expensive cigars clamped in the corner of his mouth Mr. Ely Sholter sat at his desk in his comfortable office at the Fleet Taxi Company's garage and dealt with such business as came to his hand. There was quite a lot of it, for it was nearing eight o'clock in the evening and his busy period had commenced. The cabs that had been out on the streets all day were returning by ones and twos, their drivers bringing with them reports which the fat man had to consider and sift before his unknown employer put through his nightly telephone call.

A great deal of the information that came to him was valueless, but among the mass of useless material he occasionally came across a ripe and juicy plum. It was in this way that he had discovered that the two hundred thousand pounds in paper currency was being brought from the Bank of England to the Westland Bank for lodgement in that establishment's vault over the weekend. The manager had incautiously mentioned the fact to his cashier while the two were being driven in one of the Fleet cabs. The driver had brought back the information to the garage in Waterloo Road, and Mr. Sholter had relayed it the same night to the unknown.

Up to now nothing of any importance had come in. He glanced disparagingly at the sheaf of notes on the desk before him and frowned. It looked as though it was going to be a bad day. By his instructions half a dozen of the red and black cabs had crawled along the embankment in the vicinity of Scotland Yard, hoping to pick up an official from that grim building who might discuss in the fancied privacy of the cab what schemes were being hatched and what steps were being taken to deal with the shop robberies. But although one of the cabs had driven a grey-haired Chief Constable westwards he had been alone, and they had not yet succeeded in installing a device which could record the thoughts of a passenger.

The loud speaking telephone on his desk clicked, and Mr. Sholter mechanically picked up a pencil.

'Number six, three, nine,' said a shrill cockney voice. 'Picked up two fellers this afternoon at four o'clock in the Strand and drove 'em to Victoria. Hinchcliff Stores are floatin' a new issue. They've increased their profits by seventy-five-thousand.'

Mr. Sholter scribbled a note on his pad as the telephone became silent. That was worth knowing. It might not interest his employer, but he would phone his broker in the morning and instruct him to buy as many Hinchcliff shares as he could. Mr. Sholter was never above making a little money on the side.

The telephone clicked again and a deeper voice spoke nasally.

'Number four, eight, seven, two. Cranleighs, the jewellers, have just got a special selection of emeralds in for a client of theirs. The manager of the shop was tellin' a friend of his that they're the finest stones he's ever seen.'

Mr. Sholter made another note. That was an item of information worth knowing.

For some time the loud speaking telephone remained silent, and the stout man occupied his time with his own thoughts. So far everything was going smoothly, without a hitch, but how long would it continue to do so? The police were not fools. Their organisation was every bit as efficient as the one which Mr. Sholter was connected with, and sooner or later they would hit on something that would lead them to the truth. He had carried out the orders of the unknown with regard to the bombing of the 'Q' car in Shardiloes Road, but he had carried them out under protest. In his opinion it was a false move, and, so far as he could see, an unnecessary move. This man Lake was not in any way dangerous, and it seemed to him unnecessary to have attempted his life. He had expressed his opinion, but the other had refused to listen.

'Those are my orders,' he said curtly.

'See that they're carried out. Lake will be at the bottom of Shardiloes Road at ten o'clock.'

The man Mr. Sholter had selected for the task was a Pole called Dronski, and it had been due to nobody's fault that the scheme had failed. The unknown, however, had been furious, and Ely had spent an uncomfortable five minutes while he listened to his recriminations.

The loud speaking telephone woke to life again and he broke off his thoughts abruptly to listen.

'Number nine, double six, five,' said a thin, husky voice. 'I got a bit of good news, Guv'nor. I picked up two fellers in Whitehall from the Treasury. On the twenty-seventh they're sending three million pounds to France by air from Croydon. The money's leavin' at midnight in a special aeroplane in charge of a pilot and an armed guard.'

Mr. Sholter became suddenly very alert. His pencil moved rapidly over the writing pad in front of him, and with his other hand he pressed a button. Picking up the house telephone he waited and after a short interval Billing's voice reached his ears.

'Send number nine, double six, five to me,' ordered Mr. Sholter, and replaced the telephone on its rack.

Leaning back in his chair he waited for the arrival of the man he had sent for. This last item of news was of tremendous importance. Mr. Sholter could not quite see how it could be turned to their advantage, but that was a matter to be left to the ingenuity of his employer. The fact remained that at midnight on the twenty-seventh three million pounds would be at Croydon Aerodrome for dispatch to France.

There came a tap at the door and a short, stout man dressed in the uniform the Fleet Taxi Company supplied to all their drivers, entered the office.

'Tell me some more about this money for France,' said Mr. Sholter curtly.

'There ain't much more I can tell yer, Guv'nor,' said the newcomer. 'I've told yer all I heard.'

'What form is it going in, gold or currency?' asked Ely.

The other shook his head.

'I don't know,' he answered. 'They mentioned something about bullion.'

'Then it's going in gold.' Mr. Sholter removed the cigar from his mouth and whistled softly. 'Three million pounds in gold! That'll weigh a bit.'

'They mentioned the weight,' said the driver. 'Because one of the fellers seemed doubtful if one machine'd be able to carry it. But the other said they'd spoken to one of the officials at Croydon and they was usin' one of their latest and biggest machines.'

Mr. Sholter made a rapid calculation on his pad.

'Gold to that value'd weigh something in the region of fifteen to sixteen tons,' he said.

He questioned the driver for twenty minutes, but the man could give him no further information.

When he was again alone he dropped the butt of his cigar into an ash tray, lighted another and leaning back in his chair fixed his eyes on the ceiling. Sixteen tons of gold! Something worth getting, and it would need some getting, too! It would be next to impossible to make any attempt on it during the journey from the Bank of England to Croydon. That would probably be by road and the bullion van would, without any doubt, be well guarded. That left Croydon itself, during the transit, or when the aeroplane landed in France.

Mr. Sholter racked his brains to try to discover a plan by which the gold could be successfully stolen, and at the end of half an hour he was forced to admit that he could think of nothing feasible. It was not his business anyway, but he would have liked to have had a cut and dried scheme to suggest to the unknown when he rang up.

There was a large streak of vanity in Mr. Sholter's make-up. It was beyond the capacity of his brain, however, and he gave it up and turned his attention to the numerous tasks that awaited him.

At ten o'clock coffee and sandwiches were brought to him and he drank the steaming fluid and munched his frugal meal. At intervals the loud-speaking telephone supplied him with items of information, but none of them contained anything of much importance, although he noted each item carefully down, for the man who employed him liked to receive a full report.

It was a little after eleven when the ringing of the telephone bell warned him that the unknown was coming through. Picking up the receiver he put it to his ear and heard the familiar soft, husky voice.

'Well, what's the news?' it enquired.

'Promising,' answered Mr. Sholter, and drawing his pad towards him went through item by item.

His listener made no comment until he came to the gold consignment which he had kept till the last.

'That is worth thinking about,' said the voice. 'The twenty-seventh is the date you say? That's a fortnight from now, there should be plenty of time.'

'It's almost an impossible job — ' began Mr. Sholter, but the other interrupted him.

'Nothing is impossible,' he said smoothly. 'Provided you give your mind to it. We'll go after that and we'll get it.'

Mr. Sholter went home comparatively early that night, and his sleep was broken by dreams of immense bars of gold which a man without a face was forcing him to pile, one on the top of the other, until they formed a ladder which reached up to the stars.

# 13

## Fay Obeys Instructions

Penelope Hayes read the letter which had reached her by the midday post twice, and her eyes were thoughtful beneath her drawn brows. She was a little disappointed at the contents, and yet the information that had reached her was better than she had expected. Slowly she folded the cheap sheet of notepaper and put it back in its envelope. It was unreasonable, she thought, to expect things to move quicker than they were. After all, she had achieved remarkable results in so short a time.

Going over to the big mirror set in one wall of her room she examined herself critically. She certainly did not look like a criminal she thought. No one would ever suspect the years spent in that ghastly prison.

Her thoughts turned to Arnold Lake

and she made a grimace at her reflection. What would he think if he knew the truth. She tried to imagine the expression of his face, and smiled. She could visualise the raised eyebrows and horrified astonishment.

Swiftly she passed a powder puff over her face, and leaving her room went down in the lift and entered the big dining room. Over her solitary lunch she reviewed certain things that had to be attended to. The man who acted as her agent was waiting for fresh instructions, and it was necessary that these should reach him at the earliest possible moment.

She ate leisurely. Once her eyes strayed to a girl seated at a table near her, a solitary luncher like herself, and mechanically and almost subconsciously her eyes took in the details of the smart little hat and trim costume, the pretty baby face . . .

Fay Langley saw that she was being observed, and her expression was demure. So this was the girl she was to get acquainted with. She rather liked her appearance. She experienced a little pang as she thought of what lay in store for her. This was the second time she had lunched at the Park Hotel in the hope of catching a glimpse of Penelope Hayes, but on the first occasion the girl had had her meal out and Fay Langley had merely wasted her time.

Penelope was sipping her coffee when Fay rose, having paid her bill, and passed close to the girl's table on her way to the door. The stumble she achieved was most artistically done, and putting out her hand to save herself she upset the half filled cup of coffee across the snowy cloth.

'Oh, my dear, I'm so sorry,' she apologised. 'I do hope none of that has gone over you?'

Her eyes were wide with consternation, and Penelope smiled reassuringly.

'It hasn't touched me,' she declared, and then as she saw the wide eyes narrow and an expression of pain come into the other's face she went on quickly. 'Have your hurt yourself?'

'I'm afraid I've given my ankle a twist,' said Fay untruthfully. 'I don't think it's

154

anything serious. It will be better in a minute.' She sank down in a chair and stooping rubbed ruefully at her silk clad instep. 'I'm terribly sorry,' she murmured. 'I'm afraid I'm being an awful nuisance.'

'Don't be silly, you couldn't help it,' said Penelope. 'I did the same thing going down the steps one day. It's horribly painful.'

'I hope I shall be able to walk,' said Fay. 'I have an appointment with my dressmaker in twenty minutes.'

'I shouldn't try if your ankle is very painful,' broke in Penelope practically. 'One of the waiters can 'phone and postpone your appointment.'

'I'm going to keep it if I can,' said Fay and got to her feet with the help of the chair-back. She winced artistically as she put the supposedly injured foot to the ground. 'I'm afraid I shall have to rest it for a bit,' she said in dismay. 'Oh, that is a nuisance!'

She bit her lip and sank back into the chair.

'Why not come into the lounge?' suggested Penelope. 'You'll be more comfortable there.'

The other girl agreed a little reluctantly, and with Penelope's help hobbled out of the dining room and across the vestibule into the spacious lounge. Here Penelope settled her in a deep armchair and took the one beside her.

'Which ankle is it?' she asked sympathetically.

'It's the right one,' answered Fay and extended her leg in its diaphanous stocking.

'It doesn't look as if it's swelling,' said Penelope, eyeing the injured limb critically, 'so I don't think you could have sprained it. Perhaps it's only a bad wrench.'

'I hope so,' said Fay. 'Perhaps if I sit here for a little while it'll get all right.' She opened her bag and took out a thin platinum cigarette case. 'Will you have a cigarette?' she asked holding it out to her companion.

Penelope took one and accepted a light from the little lighter that matched the cigarette case.

'Do you often come here?' asked Fay

when they were both smoking.

'I live here,' answered Penelope.

'Oh, do you? Do you prefer an hotel to a flat?'

'I'm looking for a flat,' said Penelope, 'but I haven't found one yet that suits me. In the meanwhile this place is very convenient.'

She was trying to make up her mind about this girl whose acquaintance had been accidentally forced on her. Studied at close quarters there was a certain hardness beneath the baby prettiness which warned her that she was not quite so unsophisticated as she looked.

'I live in Kensington,' Fay prattled on. 'I've got a flat in Manson Mansions. I think it's rather a ducky little place.'

She chattered on gaily, describing the colour scheme she had chosen, and she radiated such an air of childish enthusiasm that Penelope found herself growing more and more to like her. She had been very lonely since she had arrived in England, for she knew no one except the people she was employing, and they were hardly the type she could make friends with.

'I'm glad now I stumbled,' said Fay ingenuously. 'Otherwise I wouldn't have met you. It's the luckiest accident that's ever happened to me.'

'I'm rather glad, too,' said Penelope. 'You see, I've lived in America most of my life and I don't know anyone over here.'

'Oh, how dreadful!' exclaimed Fay, her eyes large with surprise. 'Haven't you any friends?'

Penelope shook her head.

'What do you do with yourself?' the other continued. 'Don't you get very bored always being alone?'

'I do at times,' said Penelope. 'But I read a lot and I'm out most of the day.'

'You must come and see me,' said Fay, breathing a silent prayer for this Heaven-sent opportunity. 'Come and have some tea one afternoon and I'll show you the flat, and all the bits and pieces I've got together.'

She was a shrewd girl, and she had formed a quick judgment of Penelope's character. That ought to fetch her, she thought to herself.

'That's very nice of you. I'd like to come,' said Penelope simply.

'Come on Thursday,' suggested Fay, and Penelope accepted her invitation.

They chatted until nearly four and then Fay announced that she thought her ankle was sufficiently recovered to enable her to walk.

'Don't forget, I shall expect you at four o'clock on Thursday,' said Fay as Penelope accompanied her to the vestibule and the commissionaire signalled to a passing taxi.

'I won't forget,' said Penelope, and watched the slim, dainty figure as it tripped down the steps and got into the waiting cab.

Fay waved to her as the taxi moved off and settled back in a corner of the seat with an expression on her face that was not entirely one of satisfaction. She had no relish for the task that lay in front of her, particularly now that she had met the girl who was to be her victim. For, strange as it may seem, she had taken an almost instant liking to Penelope Hayes, and but for the threat which Mr. Sholter had so blandly held over her head if she failed to carry out his instructions, would have refused to have anything more to do with the unsavoury business. But her motto was Fay Langley first, last, and all the time, and although she regretted the necessity she had no intention of shirking her responsibility. She had agreed to a certain action and she would carry out her promise. When Penelope Hayes came to the flat in Manson Mansions on the following Thursday afternoon she would leave it with a headache. For a destination, that all things considered, Fay felt happier she had not inquired into too closely.

# 14

## The Burglar

The man who stood in the shadow of the narrow alley almost opposite to number ten Viddle Street had caused a great deal of uneasiness to the residents of that drab and gloomy road. He had arrived with the coming of dusk and had been seen by more than one furtive eye from behind the grimy panes of the small windows. He had not the appearance of a 'busy,' but you never could tell these days when Scotland Yard recruited its men from all classes of society.

A drizzle of rain was falling and there was a cold wind which caused the watcher to draw his shabby coat closer about his thin form. For hours he had stood there, his eyes never leaving the blistered door of number ten, but he had seen no sign of Mr. Barney Gore return to his abode. That mysterious man had gone out just after the arrival of the spy, and if he had seen the watcher he had taken no notice. Neither had the man made any attempt to follow him.

An hour after he had left the house a postman had come slowly down Viddle Street and put a letter through the box of number ten. The man in the alley saw this with satisfaction and made a mental note.

It was nearing midnight and Viddle Street had reached a stage of melancholy desolation when a second man turned into the street and came slowly towards the watcher in the alley. At this hour the dubious residents were either out on their illicit business or in bed and alseep, for not a light showed from any of the dingy windows.

The newcomer noted that the blinds of Gore's house were all drawn and his pinched face showed his satisfaction.

'Thought you was never comin',' said the man in the alley as the other joined him. 'You're late, ain't yer?'

'This was the time I was told,' said the pinched-faced man. 'Is 'e out?'

The watcher nodded.

'Been out for some hours,' he said. 'The postman came soon after 'e left.'

'Good!' said the other. 'You watch for his return and if he comes while I'm busy give me a whistle.'

He crossed the road, walked rapidly past number ten until he came to a side turning — a little cul-de-sac — one side of which was formed by a wall that gave access to the backyards of the houses adjoining Mr. Barney Gore's residence. During a previous survey the man had noted this and the remembrance of it had formed the basis of his plan. Glancing rapidly about him to assure himself that he was not observed he pulled himself to the top of the wall, swung his legs over and dropped noiselessly into the tiny garden on the other side.

The back yards of the Viddle Street houses were divided by tumble down fences of wooden palings, and offered no obstacle to his progress. He negotiated four of these and found himself standing in the little concrete-paved back yard of number ten. Taking a torch from his pocket he explored cautiously, playing its beam on the door and windows. He found what he sought at length — a shuttered window that obviously belonged to the kitchen.

Pocketing his torch he replaced it with a longbladed chisel and skilfully worked on the fastening of the shutter. In less than three minutes he was climbing through the open window. Leaving it open to facilitate a hasty retreat in case of accidents, he stood in the darkness of the kitchen and listened. No sound reached him from the house and presently he began to move cautiously towards the door. It was half open, and slipping through he negotiated the narrow passage beyond and found himself in the hall.

His torch came into action again, and by its light he saw the oblong shape of a letter lying on the dusty boards by the front door. He picked it up and looked at the superscription. It was addressed to 'Barney Gore, Esq., 10 Viddle Street, Deptford.'

The envelope was of good quality; the writing obviously feminine.

With a grunt of satisfaction he carried

it back to the kitchen. There was a stained and rusty gas stove in one corner and on this stood a kettle. Carrying it into the scullery he partially filled it with water, put it back on the stove, and lit the gas. When it was boiling he held the flap of the envelope in the steam that gushed from the spout. After a second or two the gum melted and carefully he peeled the envelope open. Taking out the letter it contained he read it eagerly and producing a shabby notebook carefully copied the contents.

When he had done this and returned the book to his pocket he replaced the letter in the envelope and re-sealed it. Laying it on the table he turned out the gas, emptied the kettle, and put it back where he had found it. Then picking up the letter he replaced that, too, by the front door. Then he turned his attention to the rest of the house.

Most of the rooms were unfurnished, but presently he reached the upstairs front room in which Mr. Barney Gore seemed to spend most of his time. Rapidly he made a search of this apartment, but apparently found nothing to interest him.

Returning to the ground floor he passed along the passage to the kitchen and climbing out through the open window closed it and carefully fastened the wooden shutter as he had found it.

A quarter of an hour after he had left the house he was in a public call-box and reporting to the interested man at the other end of the wire all that he had learned.

\* \* \*

Mr. Barney Gore arrived at his abode unusually late that night, and profiting by his previous experience kept a sharp lookout for anybody who might be lurking about the vicinity of his house. Nobody knew better than he the danger he was in. He had carried his life in his hands ever since he had undertaken this project, but the watcher in the narrow alley had disappeared and Viddle Street was deserted.

Letting himself into the gloomy house

and carefully bolting the door behind him he struck a match and the first thing he saw was the letter. Picking it up he glanced at it, put it in his pocket and then went through the same procedure as he had done before. Only this time he searched the entire house, kitchen, scullery, back room, front room, coal cellar, and so to the upper floor, and he searched it with his automatic ready in his hand.

Outside his room was a trapdoor that led to the roof and getting a chair he felt the padlock that secured this. When he had assured himself that it had not been tampered with he went into his room, took the letter from his pocket of his coat and was in the act of slitting it open when he noticed the slight dampness of the flap. His heavy brows contracted and his thick lips set. Somebody had been in the house! Somebody had found that letter and read it!

With narrowed eyes he stared at the envelope thoughtfully, and then laying it on the table unopened he took out his big automatic. Pulling out the magazine he examined every cartridge carefully, tested the trigger and slipping the magazine back in the butt pulled back the jacket, throwing a cartridge into the chamber, and pushed up the safety catch. Not until he had completed these precautions did he open the letter.

He read it interestedly twice, and its contents were not reassuring. If this had been read his danger had been increased a thousand fold.

He put letter and envelope into his pocket, went over to the cupboard where he kept pen, ink, and paper, and bringing these back to the table sat himself down and wrote slowly and laboriously. When he had finished he read through what he had written, folded the two sheets, put them into an envelope and licked down the flap. Yawning he rose, took from the cupboard where he kept his writing materials an alarm clock, and set it for half past six.

Then once more examining his pistol he took off his boots, loosened his belt, and putting the automatic under the pillow, lay down on the bed and covered himself with a rug. The room was in complete darkness, not even the rays of the street lamp penetrated the thick blind that covered the window.

He was a light sleeper and the faint sound of a creaking board woke him. He lifted himself up in bed, trying to avoid making the slightest noise, and sat tensely for some minutes straining his ears. The sound that had disturbed him came again, the unmistakable sound of a footfall on the landing. He jerked aside the rug and stepped lightly to the floor. Stooping, he took his automatic from under the pillow and thumbed back the safety catch.

He could hear no sound now, and pressed against the wall he waited expectantly, every faculty alert. So much time elapsed before any further sound of movement reached him, that he began to think he had been mistaken, and then there came to his ears the sound of breathing, repressed and irregular.

The fingers of his outstretched hand were lightly touching the panels of the door and he felt it move under his touch.

Slowly it began to open, inch by inch, and he held his breath. Wider and wider it swung, and he sensed rather than saw the man who came into the room.

# 15

## Tea for Two

Thursday came and Fay Langley set about her preparations for the forthcoming tea party with no very great enthusiasm. She had telephoned the result of her meeting with Penelope Hayes to Mr. Sholter, and that gentleman had expressed his entire approval.

'You always were a clever kid,' he said admiringly. 'I knew if it was left to you you'd fix it, Fay. What time is the girl coming?'

Fay told him.

'I'll be there half an hour before she arrives,' he said. 'Don't forget to send your maid out for the afternoon.'

When the girl was told that she could go to the pictures she expressed no surprise. There had been other occasions when her mistress wished to have the flat to herself, and the result had usually been an increase in the financial department of the establishment and the paying up of overdue wages supplemented by a not unsubstantial bonus, for Fay was generous when one of her coups materialised.

'You understand,' she said when she called the maid into the dainty sitting room after lunch. 'You are not to come back before six.'

'Very well, Miss,' said the girl, rather pleased than otherwise at the prospect of an afternoon of freedom, for there was a new film at the adjacent picture house which she wanted to see.

When she had the flat to herself Fay occupied her time in preparations for her visitor's arrival. She had sent for some cakes, and the thin sandwiches she cut with her own hand.

At half past three Mr. Sholter arrived. Fay opened the door to admit him and discovered that he was accompanied by a burly, unpleasant-looking man, and that they had brought with them an American trunk.

'What's that for?' she asked.

'You'll see in good time, Fay,' said Mr.

Sholter genially. 'In the meantime we'll put it in your bedroom.'

Under his instructions the man with him picked up the trunk and carried it through into the room he had mentioned.

'Now,' said Mr. Sholter. 'You know what you've got to do, don't you, Fay? Slip a couple of drops from that bottle I gave you into her tea. It's tasteless and she won't notice anything.'

'I'll bet she notices a lot when she wakes up,' said Fay. 'I hate doing this, Sholter. It's a dirty business and I wish you hadn't asked me.'

'Forget it!' said Mr. Sholter with a movement of his plump hand. 'I've told you before that no harm will come to the girl.'

'You've told me a lot of things,' said Fay, 'but that doesn't say I believe them.' A sudden thought struck her. 'You're not going to stay here all the time are you?' she asked.

Mr. Sholter nodded.

'That was my idea,' he said, 'I thought we could sit quietly in your bedroom until — well, until after the girl had fallen asleep.'

'Well, you can't,' said Fay decidedly. 'And I'll tell you why. I promised this girl I'd show her over the flat, and if there's a room I can't take her into she might get suspicious.'

Mr. Sholter frowned.

'That's awkward,' he admitted. 'Yes, I suppose you're right.' He thought for a moment. 'What time are you having tea?' he asked.

'Oh, round about half past four, I suppose,' said Fay.

'That's all right then,' he said and his face cleared. 'I'll come back at a quarter to five. Don't forget, everything must be ready by then.'

'I won't forget,' said Fay. 'And now you'd better go. The girl may be here at any moment and you don't look the sort of man that respectable young ladies would receive without a chaperon.'

Mr. Sholter grinned, and accompanied by his unpleasant companion took his departure.

Penelope did not arrive until nearly a quarter past four, and Fay was beginning to get a little anxious, when the bell rang.

'I was afraid you weren't coming, my dear,' she said as she opened the door. 'Come in and take your things off. You'll have to excuse me if I get tea, but my maid has had to go out. Her sister has been taken ill or something and she asked if she could go and see her. It's a great nuisance, but I couldn't very well refuse. It's such a pity that servants have relations, don't you think?'

She led the way into her pretty bedroom and Penelope took off her coat and hat.

'Now, while the kettle's boiling,' said Fay, 'I'll show you round the place.'

She conducted her visitor on a tour of the flat, and showed her its appointments with pride. And the pride was genuine, for Fay had a streak of domesticity and was proud of her home.

Penelope admired everything, and her admiration was not the outcome of politeness. She thought the flat was charming and most tastefully furnished and said so candidly.

By the time they had come back to the sitting room a soft whistle from the kitchen announced the fact that the kettle was boiling, and Fay hurried away to make the tea. She returned in a few minutes pushing the laden wagon.

She chattered away inconsequently as she filled the fragile cups, and if there was a touch of feverishness in her conversation Penelope noticed nothing.

'Sugar?' she asked, and the other girl shook her head.

'No, thank you,' she replied. 'What lovely sandwiches.'

'I made them myself,' said Fay. 'I'm so glad you like them.'

The first cup of tea she handed to her guest was innocuous. She had no knowledge as to how long the effects of the drops Mr. Sholter had given her would last, and she didn't want Penelope to recover before that gentleman had put in an appearance.

'Did you have any trouble with your ankle?' asked Penelope as she sipped her tea.

For a moment Fay looked blank.

'Ankle?' she repeated, and suddenly remembered, 'Oh, no,' she said quickly. 'It was quite all right. I think the rest did it good.'

Penelope nibbled a cake which her hostess pressed on her, and Fay, with one eye on the clock, suggested another cup of tea.

The little bottle containing the knock-out drops she had slipped under the cushion of her chair and as she emptied the dregs of Penelope's cup into the slop-basin she casually distracted the girl's attention to a print that hung on the wall behind her.

'That's rather a nice specimen, I think,' she said. 'I don't know whether you're interested in such things.'

Penelope wasn't, but she politely turned her head to look at the little framed picture and by the time she looked away again a generous portion of the contents of the bottle lay at the bottom of her cup. Fay added milk and filled it with tea.

'There you are, dear,' she said. 'Will you have another sandwich?'

Penelope shook her head.

'No, thank you,' she answered.

'But you've scarcely eaten anything,' said Fay. 'You must have another of these cakes.'

But Penelope declined and sipped her tea. She thought it tasted a little bitter, but put this down to the fact that it had been standing in the silver tea-pot, and had no suspicion as to the true reason for that faintly unpleasant taste.

The hands of the clock were almost on the quarter to five, and Fay began to wonder whether she had left it too late. To her relief she saw Penelope drink her tea and set down the empty cup.

'I — ' she began, and Fay saw her face change. The colour receded, leaving it white, and her eyes suddenly became dazed and glassy.

'My dear, what's the matter?' she said leaning forward with simulated concern.

Penelope tried to speak, but only a vague sound issued from her lips. She half rose from her chair, swayed, and with a little groan fell back limply. She was so pale and looked so ill that Fay was frightened. Had she overdone the dose? In her hurry she might have been a little careless . . .

She got up and went over to the unconscious girl, peering down at her anxiously. She was breathing stertorously through parted lips and Fay was a little relieved. Penelope's head had fallen sideways and taking a cushion from the settee she slipped it behind her, shifting her into a more comfortable position.

She had scarcely done this when the bell rang, and hurrying out to the hall she admitted Mr. Sholter and his unpleasant-looking friend.

'Everything all right, Fay?' he asked anxiously, and she sniffed.

'If you call it all right, yes,' she answered curtly. 'She's gone off, if that's what you mean.'

'What else should I mean,' said Mr. Sholter, and rubbed his plump hands with satisfaction.

'Go and fetch that trunk, Stevens.'

His companion nodded and disappeared into the bedroom while Mr. Sholter accompanied Fay to the sitting room. He went straight over to the chair in which Penelope reclined and stared down at her.

'Useful stuff, Butyl,' he remarked. 'Swift, and the after-effects are not too

179

unpleasant. What did you do with the bottle?'

Fay had slipped it back under the cushion of the chair after administering the dose and now retrieved it, holding it out to him.

'I'd better take this,' he said suiting the action to the word, and then as he looked at the contents his thick lips pursed. 'You didn't spare the dose!' he exclaimed. 'You've been pretty extravagant with the stuff.'

'There's no danger is there?' asked Fay a little scared.

He shook his head.

'No, there's no danger,' he answered. 'But it'll be a long time before she comes round. Perhaps that'll be an advantage, though.'

The man called Stevens came in at that moment staggering under the weight of the trunk.

'Bring it over here,' ordered Mr. Sholter, and the man put it down beside the unconscious girl's chair.

When it was opened Fay saw that the inside had been padded, and guessed the reason.

'You're not going to put her in there?' she cried in dismay. 'Why, she'll suffocate!'

'She'll do nothing of the sort,' retorted Mr. Sholter. 'She'll get plenty of air. That trunk has been specially prepared for the purpose, and if you look closely you can see that a number of holes have been bored.'

Fay said nothing more, but watched as they lifted the limp form of Penelope and put her in the trunk. When it was closed Mr. Sholter took a bunch of keys from his pocket and locked it.

'There we are,' he said. 'Everything nice and comfy, and not a hitch. Go and call up the taxi driver, Stevens.'

The surly-looking man departed and when he had gone Mr. Sholter put his hand in his breast pocket and took out a big wad of notes.

'The labourer is worthy of his hire,' he said as he handed them to Fay.

She hesitated for a moment before taking them.

'I feel like Judas,' she muttered.

'You look like an angel,' he answered

gallantly. 'You've carried the thing through very well, Fay. Perhaps we'll be able to find you some more little jobs equally as profitable.'

'You can keep them,' said the girl briefly. 'I don't want any more jobs like this, thank you. I'm not a saint, but I draw the line at some things.'

Mr. Sholter shrugged his fat shoulders.

'That's as you please,' he said. 'Personally I think you're foolish to throw away the chance of making good money.'

The man Stevens came back at that moment accompanied by another man in the uniform of the Fleet Taxi Company.

'Take the trunk down to the cab,' said Mr. Sholter.

They picked it up between them and carried it out to the front door. As he was preparing to follow them the fat man looked back.

'Don't forget to wash that cup, Fay,' he warned, and as he crossed the threshold she slammed the front door in his face.

The other two men were staggering down the stairs with the trunk and Mr. Sholter, who disliked unnecessary exercise, stepped into the lift. He reached the vestibule before they did and waited. Presently they appeared, and he stood watching while the trunk was carried out to a taxi standing outside the entrance and carefully strapped on the platform beside the driver's seat. The surly faced man got in and the driver took his place behind the wheel. Out of the corner of his eye Mr. Sholter saw a policeman approaching.

'Euston,' he said in a loud voice so that it would reach the ears of the man in blue, and sprang into the cab beside his companion.

As it moved off the constable glanced casually at the big trunk in front and passed on his leisurely way, never dreaming that he had witnessed the abduction of a girl who had in her possession information his superiors at Scotland Yard would have given much to obtain.

# 16

## The Raid on Cranleigh's

Cranleigh's occupies a corner site at the junction of Old Bond Street with New Bond Street. The exterior is not very imposing, but Cranleigh's has a reputation among those people who are connoisseurs of jewels, and their clients number some of the richest people in the world. In the big vault below the shop is often to be found a small fortune in stones and knowing this the police have special instructions regarding Cranleigh's. A night watchman is kept on the premises, occupying a little office whose barred window overlooks the side street, and it is the duty of the patrol to receive an 'All well' signal from this man every hour during the night. A dim light burns constantly in the office room and it is possible for the constable on the beat to see the watchman as he sits at his vigil.

It was a dark night and rain was falling heavily when Police Constable Tenning came majestically down Old Bond Street shining his lantern on the fastenings of the various doors as he passed.

It was a little after two when he reached Cranleigh's corner and turning into the side street made his way to the barred window to exchange his usual signal with the watchman. The dim light was burning as usual and the watchman was sitting at his table reading a newspaper. Tenning tapped on the window and flashed his light and the man raised his head and waved reassuringly. Tenning continued on his way, his measured footfall fading in the distance, and the man who had been seated at the table dropped his newspaper and wiped his wet forehead.

'Everythin' all right?' asked a hoarse voice from the darkness of the passage outside the half closed door of the little office.

The man who had impersonated the watchman grunted an affirmative.

'I think so,' he said. 'He didn't appear to be suspicious.'

He heard a sigh of relief from his unseen companion, and then the door was pushed wider and the man came half into the small apartment.

'Me 'eart was in me marf until 'e'd gone,' he whispered. 'Though there's no reason why 'e should 'ave suspected anythin'. You're like enough to the real feller in this light to take 'im in.'

He glanced at something that lay crumpled up in the shadow of a steel filing cabinet. It was the body of the unfortunate watchman and the surprise which had come to his face when he died was still there, for he had been struck down by one whom he had every reason to regard as a friend, the man in the policeman's uniform who now stood leaning against the door jamb looking at him critically. He had tapped on the window ten minutes before the real patrolman was due and had signalled for the watchman to open the door, the side door that gave admittance to the back of the premises. The unsuspecting man had obeyed, for it was not unusual for him to pass the tedious hours chatting for a few moments to one of the constables on duty. It was against his orders, and in this instance had led to his death, for barely had he opened the door when the pseudo-policeman had struck him savagely on the head, and his interest in Cranleigh's and everything else had departed for ever.

'How long are those fellers downstairs goin' to be?' asked the man who had taken his place.

'Harry said it'd take him a couple of hours to cut through the door,' answered the other.

'That means the rozzer'll be round again,' muttered his companion. 'He comes round every hour.'

'Well, you ain't got anythin' to worry about,' the uniformed man assured him. 'If 'e didn't suspect nothin' the first time it ain't likely 'e will the second.'

'It's all very well for you — ' began the other.

'Is it!' snapped the man by the door. 'It's an 'anging job for me. I wish now I 'adn't 'it that bloke so 'ard.'

Had he been able to see what Police

Constable Tenning was doing at that moment he might have wished this even more fervently, for Tenning was by no means as unsuspicious as they believed.

It was quite a small thing that had aroused in his mind a feeling of uneasiness. When the supposed watchman had given his reassuring wave he had seen that he was wearing a wristwatch. This was peculiar, for he knew that his friend the watchman at Cranleigh's carried a large and bulky silver watch in his pocket which had been presented to him by the men of the Nineteenth Cheshires. Roots, the watchman, was very proud of that watch and hardly likely to have discarded it in favour of one of the wrist variety.

Tenning wondered, and, wondering, made up his mind on his course of action. There might be nothing in it, but at the same time he wasn't going to take the responsibility. If there *was* anything wrong at Cranleigh's it wouldn't be much good trying to cope with it himself. Very sensibly, as it turned out, he decided to telephone his station and mention his suspicion to the Divisional Inspector.

There was a call box in Oxford Street and from here he put his call through.

The inspector, who had heard all about the Westland Bank robbery and the cleaning out of the jewellers' shops, took a serious view of the situation.

'You did quite right to ring up, Tenning,' he said. 'I'll rush up some men and surround the place. Don't do anything until I get there unless anyone attempts to leave. I'll meet you at the Oxford Street end of New Bond Street.'

Tenning left the box rather elated at his foresight, and fervently hoping that he had not dragged the inspector and a squad of men out on a wild goose chase.

The rain was still falling heavily, and in spite of the fact that his action had been commended, if nothing came of it the inspector would not relish a soaking, and might naturally feel a little irritated.

It was ten minutes before the long police car put in an appearance and drew up to the sidewalk. The Divisional Inspector was the first to alight and greeted Tenning as the constable approached him.

'Anything happened?' he asked.

'No, sir,' said Tenning. 'I haven't been back to the shop but I can see both exits from a little way up New Bond Street and nobody has attempted to leave.'

The inspector grunted his satisfaction. He had brought six men with him, and under his direction they began to move noiselessly towards the premises of Cranleigh's. Less than two minutes after the arrival of the tender a cordon had been established round the shop.

The light was still burning dimly in the office room behind the barred window and accompanied by Tenning the inspector tried the side door and hammered with his fist on the panel. There was no reply to his knocking but he thought he heard a movement somewhere inside.

'Go and look through the window and see if you can still see the watchman,' he whispered, and Tenning obeyed.

But even as he reached it the light went out. Almost at the same instant the side door was jerked open and a man rushed out.

'Here, I want you,' cried the inspector,

but his voice was drowned in the loud explosion of an automatic as the man jerked up his arm and fired at point blank range.

The inspector ducked and the bullet went past him, smashing the window of a shop on the opposite corner. The man fired again, and this time the inspector went down with a bullet in his leg.

Three other men came tearing out of the narrow doorway, each carrying a pistol. Tenning saw that one was dressed in the uniform of a policeman, but without a helmet.

The detectives who had been stationed round the shop came hurriedly at the sound of the shots, but as they approached, the four robbers opened fire and they were greeted by a fusillade of bullets that checked their advance. Two went down, writhing, on the pavement, and Tenning made a grab at the man in uniform. He received a smashing blow from the butt of the pistol full in his face and staggered backwards half blinded with pain.

The four men went racing down New Bond Street, spraying their pursuers with bullets as they ran. Four of the men were wounded, two of them severely. The remainder continued gamely to give chase, but the thieves had got a good start, and they were more than a hundred yards ahead when they reached the broad thoroughfare of Oxford Street.

A crawling taxi came into view and into this they tumbled, firing a final volley through the window as it sped away towards the Circus.

The driver of the police tender, hearing the sound of the shots, had got down to come to the assistance of his comrades, but seeing what was happening, he hurried back to his machine and it was moving in the wake of the taxi when the two C.I.D. men who remained uninjured reached it.

'Four men in that taxi!' panted the foremost. 'See if you can catch them.'

The police driver needed no urging. The powerful car leaped forward in pursuit of the red tail lamp of the fleeing taxi. But luck was in favour of the escaping men. The police car would almost certainly have overtaken them but for the fact that a stray bullet burst the off side front tyre and brought its speed down to a crawl.

The police driver brought his machine to a forced standstill and cursed volubly as he saw the red tail light of his quarry disappear in the distance.

The noise of the shooting had attracted attention and even at that hour a small crowd had gathered. They were pressing curiously round the police car when three uniformed men came up at a run.

'What's the matter here?' demanded a policeman roughly. 'Who fired them shots?'

One of the plain clothes men muttered something to him and the man's demeanour changed.

'Sorry, sir,' he said. 'I thought you might be responsible, seeing the crowd round the car.'

The Divisional Inspector came limping down New Bond Street. The wound in his leg was painful but not serious. The bullet had passed through the fleshy part of his calf, and an improvised bandage made from his handkerchief had checked the bleeding.

He demanded to know what had happened, and when he was told his face was stern.

'Armed thieves are a new one on me,' he grunted. 'Tell one of those men to go back to the station for an ambulance, some of our fellows have been pretty seriously hurt.'

He was hurt himself, every step he took was an agony, and his face was pale and drawn, but he was a determined man. While his order was being obeyed he made his way to the call box from which Tenning had rung him. A minute later he was speaking to Scotland Yard.

The night inspector listened to his brief report, and ten minutes after it had been received the operator in the wireless room at Imber Court was calling 'All cars' of the mobile squad.

Arnold Lake, running slowly along Hammersmith Broadway received the news from his wireless operator and gave orders for the 'Q' car to proceed at full speed to New Bond Street. Tonight he carried a full crew aboard. Beside himself there was a police driver, two plain clothes men and the wireless operator. When they reached the scene of the attempted robbery they found three other cars already there and a crowd of men gathered outside the jewellery store.

'What's happened?' asked Arnold as he joined them.

The man to whom he had addressed his question looked round and he recognised Chief Inspector Chedley.

'Pretty serious,' growled that worried official, and briefly explained. 'The night watchman's dead,' he finished grimly. 'One of the divisional men has got a bullet through his stomach and it's only a question of hours. It looks like the same crowd that did the Westland Bank and the other shops, but this time they didn't get anything for their trouble if that's any consolation.'

He went into the store through the side door and Arnold followed. A doctor was bending over the body of the watchman and the Divisional Inspector, his face chalk white but grimly sticking to his job, was sitting near him.

'The man was struck savagely several

times,' said the doctor, who had evidently just completed his examination. 'A great deal of force was used and he must have died almost immediately.'

Arnold caught a glimpse of the unfortunate man's head and believed him.

Under Chedley's orders a rapid search of the premises was made, but so far as could be ascertained nothing was missing. The thieves had evidently been disturbed before they had time to more than start on the big safe in the vault below. The door leading to this was open and a complete set of the latest safe breaking implements was found scattered about on the concrete floor. There were oxy-acetylene blow pipes, cylinders of gas and everything necessary for the forcing of a modern patterned safe.

'Collect those up and test 'em for prints,' ordered Chedley, and one of the men with him nodded and began to carry out the order.

In the midst of the police investigations Mr. Cranleigh arrived. The owner of the store was an elderly, grey-haired man who looked like a retired military officer. His consternation when he heard what had happened was almost ludicrous.

'This is the first time in my experience such a thing has been attempted,' he declared. 'Cranleigh's have always congratulated themselves that they have been in existence for over a century and never had a burglary. It's a most fortunate thing that the thieves were stopped before they succeeded in opening the safe. There's nearly two hundred thousand pounds worth of picked emeralds which we have been collecting to the order of a client for the past six months.'

'Who knew about these emeralds?' asked Chedley quickly.

Mr. Cranleigh shook his head.

'Beyond my client, myself and my manager, no one,' he replied.

'What's the name of your client?' asked the Chief Inspector.

The jeweller hesitated.

'I don't know that — er — that I can tell you that,' he said doubtfully.

'I'm sorry, sir, but I must insist.' Chedley's tone was regretful but firm.

'I've no need to point out that this is a very serious business. Murder has been committed and I must insist that you withhold no information that is likely to help the police.'

'But I don't see how my client's name — ' began Mr. Cranleigh and again Chedley interrupted him.

'That is for me to decide,' he said, and the jeweller capitulated.

He mentioned an illustrious name, and Chedley raised his eyebrows.

'And your manager?' he asked. 'Is he to be trusted?'

'Most certainly!' said Mr. Cranleigh. 'Most definitely! He has been with the firm now over forty years.'

'I should like his name and address also,' said the Chief Inspector, and without hesitation this time the jeweller gave them to him.

'It's obvious,' went on the detective, 'that these people knew about the emeralds and that that's what they were after. You're quite certain you haven't mentioned the fact that they were on the premises to anyone except the two persons you have mentioned?'

Mr. Cranleigh shook his head.

'I'm positive,' he declared.

'Where have you spoken about them?' asked the Chief Inspector.

'In my private office,' said the jeweller.

'You haven't mentioned them anywhere in public?' suggested Chadley.

'No,' said Mr. Cranleigh. 'Apart from the fact that I shouldn't dream of advertising that stones to that value were on my premises the deal was more or less a confidential one. My client did not want it known until — until after a certain event.'

Chedley nodded.

'I quite understand,' he said, and he did, for the name of the client had told him all he wanted to know concerning the history of the emeralds. 'What about your staff?'

'My staff knew nothing about them,' said Mr. Cranleigh. 'But even if they had, both my assistants are reliable men and have been with the firm a number of years.'

Chedley rubbed his chin.

'Well, I can't understand how these

people knew,' he muttered. 'And they did know, that I'll swear. The same as they knew about the money in the Westland Bank. They wouldn't have undertaken this job on spec., it's been too carefully prepared. Somehow or other the fact that those emeralds were in the safe must have leaked out.' He caught sight of a peculiar expression on the jeweller's face and stopped. 'What is it?' he asked. 'You've thought of something.'

'I have,' confessed Mr. Cranleigh. 'I've just remembered that I did mention the stones to my manager, but nobody could possibly have overheard us.'

'Where?' snapped the Chief Inspector.

'In a taxi the other afternoon,' said Mr. Cranleigh. 'I had succeeded in acquiring a particular sized stone that I wanted, that morning, and I told my manager that the collection was now complete.'

'A taxi, eh?' Chedley frowned. 'H'm, that may be a valuable clue, Mr. Cranleigh. These fellows escaped in a taxi tonight. The mobile squad are combing London for it at the present moment.'

Arnold, too, was thoughtful, for it had been by means of a taxi that the attempted abduction of Penelope Hayes had been carried out.

The streets were grey with the cold light of dawn before the police investigations were over and he reported at Scotland Yard and made his tired way to his little flat. In the excitement of the night he had forgotten his luncheon appointment with the girl, but it recurred to his mind as, after leaving a note for his servant to call him at eleven-thirty, he undressed quickly preparatory to snatching a few hours' sleep. And he remembered it with mixed feelings. He was very keen on seeing Penelope again, but he had little relish for the unpleasant task he had set himself of questioning her concerning her past in America.

It troubled him so much that, tired as he was, it was some little time before he could get to sleep. He need not have worried, but he did not know that. For it was a long time before he was to see Penelope Hayes again, and when he did all questions were to prove superfluous.

# 17

Murder!

Arnold had arranged to meet Penelope in the vestibule of the Park Hotel at one, and arrived five minutes early for his appointment. There was no sign of the girl in the big foyer and seating himself on one of the lounges he waited. He had decided that he would not broach the subject that was uppermost in his mind until they had reached the coffee stage of the meal.

One o'clock came and went but no Penelope arrived. At a quarter past one, when she had still not put in an appearance, Arnold rose and strolled over to the desk clerk.

'Do you know if Miss Hayes is in?' he enquired. 'She was to meet me here at one o'clock.'

He thought the man looked at him rather queerly.

'I don't think she is in, sir,' he said. 'If you will wait one moment I'll see.'

Arnold lit a cigarette, and, turning, watched the little stream of people who were passing to and fro. He was still engaged thus when a stoutish man in an immaculate morning suit touched him on the arm.

'Excuse me,' said the newcomer. 'But are you a friend of Miss Hayes, sir?'

Arnold nodded in some surprise. He guessed that the man before him was the manager, and his guess was to be confirmed.

'I'm the manager of the hotel,' said that individual. 'I should like a word with you in private. Will you come to my office?'

He led the way across the vestibule to a polished door and opening it ushered the astonished and rather alarmed Arnold into a comfortably furnished office.

'I'm very sorry to trouble you, sir,' he said when he closed the door, 'but I should be rather glad to have your advice.'

'Concerning what?' asked the young inspector.

'Concerning Miss Hayes,' said the manager. 'She left the hotel early yesterday afternoon and has not returned.'

Arnold's alarm increased. There flashed through his mind the girl's attempted abduction on the night when he had prevented her being carried off in the taxi.

'I shouldn't have thought anything of it,' continued the manager, 'only Miss Hayes definitely left instructions with the floor waiter to have a meal served in her room at ten o'clock last night. When it was reported to me this morning that she had not returned to the hotel I was naturally a little worried. I was afraid that perhaps some sort of accident had happened to the lady, and it occurred to me that the police should be informed. I hesitated to take this step, however, in case Miss Hayes might be staying away of her own accord, in which case she would naturally resent any interference on my part. We don't like to do anything that would cause our guests any annoyance.'

He stopped and looked at Arnold, and the young inspector saw what was passing in his mind. Hesitating to take the responsibility himself he was trying to lay it on the shoulders of the missing girl's friend. If he liked to take action, then it was nothing to do with the manager, and no kick would come to the hotel if Penelope became angry at this interference in her private affairs.

Arnold came to a quick decision.

'I am a friend of Miss Hayes,' he said. 'And I am also a member of the police.'

It was the manager's turn to look astonished.

'Indeed, sir,' he said raising his eyebrows. 'In that case I'm very glad I spoke to you. Perhaps you are aware of the lady's reason for not returning?'

'I am not,' said Arnold. 'But I feel that it should be enquired into without delay. Unless she has become involved in some kind of accident I don't think she would have failed to keep her appointment with me today.'

At the back of his mind he thought there might be another explanation for the girl's absence. Had she, in some way, discovered that her past was known to him, and, afraid that he might pass this information on to headquarters, decided to disappear in order to avoid a police enquiry?

It was possible, but it didn't strike him as probable. There was no means by which the girl could have become aware of his knowledge, unless she had seen and recognised Captain Nansen when the latter had stopped him after she had driven away in the taxi.

There was another and less pleasant explanation for her absence and that was that she had fallen into the hands of the people who had attempted to kidnap her before. Whatever the reason was, it was necessary that no time should be lost in trying to ascertain her whereabouts.

'If you've no objection,' said Arnold, 'I should like to see Miss Hayes' room.'

The manager had no objection.

'I'll take you up myself,' he said, and leaving the office escorted Arnold to the lift.

They went up to the fifth floor, passed along a heavily carpeted corridor and paused outside a door on the right.

'I instructed the chambermaid to bring the key to me this morning,' said the manager taking it from his pocket. 'I thought it would be best, when it was discovered that Miss Hayes had not returned and that her bed had not been slept in, to leave the room exactly as she had left it.'

Arnold blessed the man's foresight.

Unlocking the door the manager threw it open and Arnold stepped across the threshold into the prettily furnished bedroom. A glance showed him that there was little doubt that Penelope had intended returning. Several of her things were scattered untidily about the apartment and two newish looking suitcases stood at the foot of the bed. This had obviously not been touched since it had been made on the previous day. The coverlet was turned down and the girl's nightdress lay in readiness.

'Have you any idea where she went to yesterday afternoon when she left here?' he asked.

The manager shook his head.

'No idea at all,' he replied. 'I did make

enquiries of the commissionaire and he said Miss Hayes left about half past three. He asked her if she wanted a taxi and she said no.'

Arnold rubbed his chin. The girl might have gone anywhere, there was no possible means of telling. If she had taken a taxi it would not have been difficult to trace the cab, but since she had walked it was next to impossible to follow her movements. There was always the chance that she had picked up a cab after she had left the hotel, and Arnold made a mental note to have this looked into. If she had, and the driver of the cab could be found, he would be in a position to say where he had set down his fare.

He was taking a serious view of the situation, for some instinct warned him that the girl was not staying away of her own accord.

Before the manager would allow him to search the room she had occupied he had to satisfy that cautious individual regarding his identity, and even then he insisted on remaining while the search was conducted.

Under his watchful eye Arnold began a careful examination. There was a little bureau against one wall and in this he made a discovery. Stuck in one of the compartments amongst some envelopes and stationary he found a letter. The envelope was of cheap quality and his heart jumped as he saw that the postmark was the Deptford district.

Here perhaps was a clue. The date on which the letter had been sent was three days previously, and opening the envelope he extracted the single sheet of paper which it contained. This had been torn from an inexpensive writing block and was headed '10, Viddle Street.' followed by the date.

*'Dear Madam,' it began. 'I think I have at last succeeded in discovering something definite. I believe that the man you are in search of is living in this neighbourhood, as you always suspected, although he has changed his name from the one you gave me. If I am right you will no doubt be able to recognise him. If you could meet me*

*one evening I can take you to a place*
*which he frequents and you could*
*yourself confirm my belief that I have*
*at last discovered the person you are*
*seeking. Will you answer this as soon as*
*possible and let me know when, where*
*and at what time you could meet me.*
　　　　　　　'*Yours faithfully,*
　　　　　　　　'*Barney Gore.*'

Arnold frowned. He remembered Sergeant Fisk's story of the constable of whom Penelope had asked the way to Viddle Street. Obviously she had been on her way to see this man Gore who corresponded with her. But who was the man she was seeking and whom he had apparently succeeded in discovering? That, like everything else connected with her, was a mystery, he thought irritably. Still, the letter provided him with a valuable piece of information.

Had she arranged the appointment for the previous evening and as a result become involved in some kind of trouble which had prevented her returning to the hotel? Obviously the next move was to find Mr. Barney Gore and see what he had to say.

The manager, who had been watching him curiously while he read the letter, broke into a flood of questions as Arnold folded it and replaced it in its envelope, but the young inspector replied evasively. The man's curiosity was natural in the circumstances, but he felt he had no right to satisfy it. The letter which he held in his hand was Penelope's personal property, and he had no authority to make the contents public.

He put the letter in his pocket, and, after instructing the manager to keep the girl's room locked and to allow nobody to enter it under any excuse whatever, he left the hotel and took a taxi to Meadow Lane.

Sergeant Fisk was seated in his accustomed position behind his desk and to the grizzled-haired man Arnold put a question.

'Never heard the name, sir,' answered the sergeant. 'But if he lives in Viddle Street you can take it from me that he's a crook. That place has got one of the worst reputations in the district. What's he wanted for?'

'He isn't wanted for anything at present,' said Arnold. 'I merely wanted to know if you knew anything about him.'

The desk sergeant shook his head slowly.

'Afraid I don't, sir,' he replied.

Arnold put one or two more questions, and then, leaving the station house turned his steps in the direction of Viddle Street.

At that hour of the day it was full of screaming children. A mean-looking street lined on either side by narrow, dirty, and mean-looking houses. Arnold made his way slowly along the right hand side, while the children paused in their games to eye him curiously and mutter ribald remarks to their companions.

He came to number ten and paused to look at the house. It was, if anything, a trifle meaner and more dirty-looking than its neighbours. The tattered blinds were down and there was no sign of life. The front door, like all the other front doors, opened directly on the pavement, and reaching up his hand Arnold grasped the rusty knocker and gave a sharp rat-tat.

The sound echoed hollowly within the house, but there was no reply. Arnold looked about him and discovered that he had an adult audience. From the various narrow doorways faces peered at him, unpleasant faces with small, hate-filled eyes. The inhabitants of Viddle Street had recognised one of their natural enemies — a 'busy.' Somebody made a crude jest and a discordant note of laughter rippled from mouth to mouth. A queer, unfriendly lot of people, thought Arnold, as the laughter died to an intermittent, sly, chuckling.

He turned his attention once more to the silent house. Again he knocked, and again received no answer to his summons. Perhaps Mr. Barney Gore was out or sleeping. He stooped, and regardless of his audience, peered through the narrow letter slit. Dimly he made out a bare and unfurnished passage and the beginning of a flight of carpetless stairs. He listened but there was no sound, and then as he straightened up he saw a policeman coming towards him from the other end of the street.

The man eyed him suspiciously as he drew nearer, and then as he recognised Arnold his face cleared.

'Any trouble, sir?' he asked.

'Not in the way you mean,' said the young inspector. 'But I want to have a word with the man who lives at number ten, and I can't make him hear.'

'Perhaps he ain't in,' suggested the constable.

'Very likely not,' agreed Arnold.

'It's a curious thing,' went on the man, 'but I was only talkin' to that feller a few nights ago. Two chaps was 'angin' about outside the front of his house, and he was leanin' out his window talkin' to them. From the tone of his voice I thought there was some trouble afoot, and I asked him if anythin' was the matter. A little while after I 'eard shootin' over in that alley.' He jerked his head to the alley opposite. 'But when I got there I couldn't find nothin'. What do you want to see him for sir?'

'I think he may be in possession of information,' answered Arnold, but beyond that refused to satisfy the policeman's curiosity.

'Maybe 'e's in and won't answer,' said the man. 'Let me try.'

He grasped the knocker and beat a thunderous tattoo, and stepping back looked up at the blind-covered windows. But his efforts met with no better results than Arnold's had done.

''Fraid there's nothin' doin', sir,' he said shaking his head, and Arnold was reluctantly forced to agree.

He accompanied the man to the end of the street and here they parted. Turning into a street that ran at right angles with the one he had just left Arnold walked slowly along with knitted brows. He was tremendously worried over this disappearance of Penelope. The more he thought of it the more certain he became that the girl had got into some kind of trouble. And if this was the case, if the people who had tried to get her before had succeeded, every second wasted added to her danger. And the one man who might be able to supply some information was un-get-at-able.

He reached the end of the street he was in, stopped, hesitated, and retraced his steps. An idea had occurred to him which should not, strictly speaking, have entered the head of a representative of the law.

He remembered passing a little blind alley on the same side of Viddle Street as that of number ten. He made his way back to this and turned down it. As he had expected it gave access to the backyards of the houses adjoining the one occupied by the mysterious man he was so anxious to see.

Arnold made up his mind and decided to put the half-formed plan which had occurred to him into action. Ten minutes later he was standing in the concrete paved backyard of the house at which he had knocked so futilely a short while before. He had taken a considerable risk in negotiating the fences of the intervening yards, but apparently nobody had seen him. It was more than likely the inhabitants were far too busily occupied in discussing his presence at the front doors with their neighbours.

Examining the forbidding back of number ten he saw that a window near the back entrance was partly open. Going over to this and looking in he discovered that it gave admittance to a scullery. He gave a quick glance about him, saw that he was unobserved, and pushing the window wide swung his legs over the sill and dropped lightly into the room beyond. He was breaking the law and none knew this better than he. If the owner of the house chose to make a complaint he would be severely reprimanded by his superiors. But he had thrashed all this out in his mind before coming to his decision.

There was no sound in the house, and he entered the kitchen. The door leading into the passage which communicated with the hall was open, and presently he was standing at the foot of the stairs listening. There was silence everywhere.

From the street outside he could hear the shrill voices of the children as they played in the gutters, but from within utter silence.

'Any one at home?' he called up the bare stairway. The sound of his voice echoed but no one answered.

Cautiously he began to ascend and

found himself on a bare landing. Facing him was a partly open doorway, and going to this Arnold pushed it wide and peered in.

The room was in darkness. The tattered blind that hung over the window preventing any light from penetrating. He took a step forward and struck a match, and as the little sliver of wood flickered into a feeble yellow flame his breath whistled through his teeth sharply.

The house was not empty. It was occupied. Between the table and a narrow bed lay a sprawling heap . . .

The match burned Arnold's fingers and he dropped it. But he had seen, in that brief moment, a candle standing on the table and striking another match he lit it. As the flame burned up and dispersed the darkness he saw that the sprawling heap was the figure of a man, a man who lay outstretched, his heavy face contorted into a grin of agony. In one hand he grasped an automatic, and for a moment Arnold thought it was a case of suicide, and then he saw the knife that protruded from the chest, and altered his opinion.

The man had been murdered, and judging from the condition of the blood which soaked his clothing and which had spread in a little pool over the bare boards, had been dead for a long time. For when he put his finger to it he found that it was dry and hard.

# 18

## The Prison-House

Penelope Hayes awoke and blinked painfully, for even the dim light in the room hurt her. She felt very ill, and her mouth was dry and unpleasant. For some time she lay incapable of thought, her brain refusing to respond to anything except a physical sensation of sickness.

After a while, however, this wore off a little and memory came back to her. She remembered drinking the tea in the flat at Kensington and the terrible sensation of the room swimming round her. What had happened? Had she been taken ill, and was this a hospital?

She raised her head with difficulty and looked about her in the dim light. It came from a candle standing on the table in the centre of a small, almost square room, none too clean and containing very little furniture. A strip of threadbare carpet covered the bare boards and against one wall stood a rickety washstand with a tin basin and ewer. The window, its grimy panes protected by stout bars of iron, was innocent of curtains, but what lay beyond it was impossible to tell, for outside it was pitch dark.

She still felt dazed and sick. Her head ached dully and her eyes were hot and tired, but she was sufficiently sensible to realise that this was no hospital. Where had she been brought to?

The throbbing in her temples was so bad that she was glad to lie back on the narrow truckle bed and close her eyes. Whether she dozed or not she was unable to say, but presently when she opened them again she felt better.

Looking round she saw a towel hanging up on a hook behind the door and swinging her legs off the bed she got tremulously to her feet. A wave of dizziness overcame her and she had to hang on to the rail to support herself. It passed, and going over to the washstand she poured out some water into the basin and bathed her face and hands. When she had dried them on the towel she felt a little better.

The atmosphere of the room was stuffy and heavy. She went to the window and tried to open it, but she found that a number of screws had been driven through the sash into the frame and it was immovable. Short of breaking the glass there was no way of getting fresh air. She went to the door and tried the handle, discovering that it was locked, and then, for the first time, she guessed what had happened to her, and the knowledge sent a shiver through her spine. The tea which she had drunk must have been drugged. It was the after-effects of the drug that was making her feel so queer.

She sat wearily on one side of the bed and with her head in her hands tried to reason rationally. But her system had not yet thrown off the heavy dose of butyl which had been administered to her, and in the midst of her thoughts she must have gone to sleep, for the next thing she knew was that somebody was shaking her by the shoulders and that a brilliant light was shining in her eyes.

She sat up with a jerk and a stifled cry,

blinking into the flame of the candle held in the hand of a hard-faced woman who was a stranger to her.

'Slept it off?' growled the woman in a harsh voice. ''Ere, I've brought you some tea.'

She held out a thick cup and saucer and taking it Penelope drank the strong, over-sweetened liquid eagerly.

'Where is this place? Who brought me here?' she asked.

The woman gave her a queer look that made her unpleasant face even more unpleasant.

'Ask no questions and you'll 'ear no lies,' she answered, and turning abruptly away went out, and Penelope heard the key turn in the lock.

She was under no illusions regarding her danger. If the person whom she suspected was at the bottom of getting her to this place it was very real.

In the dim flickering light of the candle she sat thinking, and presently she found herself shivering. The room was cold since no preparation had been made for heating, and she fetched a blanket from the bed and wrapped it round her shoulders. Going over to the window she peered out into the darkness, but could see nothing. Apparently it had begun to rain for she could hear the drip, drip of water from a broken gutter and the window outside was wet. She had expected to hear the sound of traffic but everything was quiet, so quiet that she guessed she was somewhere in the country.

She had gone back to the side of the bed when suddenly the silence was shattered by a banging door from somewhere below and listening she heard steps mounting the stairs. They drew nearer, came along the landing, and paused outside her door. There was the rattle of a bunch of keys and a click as the lock turned. The door opened and a man came in.

He was of medium height with a wizened face that vice had marked with deep lines and given an age that years did not warrant. His nose was thin and reddish-coloured in strong contrast to the pale, unhealthy hue of his face, and the eyes, small and beadlike, were set so close to the bridge that they were almost lost in its shadow.

'Get up!' he ordered harshly. 'I've come to take you away.'

She tried to move, but her limbs were trembling so that they refused to obey the command of her brain. Coming over the man gripped her by the arm and jerked her roughly to her feet.

'Come with me,' he said leading her towards the door. 'And just do as you're told. If you don't it'll be the worse for you. If you try any tricks I'll cut your throat!'

He held up his hand and the light from the candle glistened on the blade of a knife. Half paralysed with terror she allowed him to take her down the stairs. He led her along a passage towards a back door and pulling back the bolts of this jerked it open.

'Out you go,' he muttered, and she stepped across the threshold into the darkness of the night.

The refreshing sting of rain lashed her face and a cool breeze blew round her head.

'This way,' muttered the man, and clasping her arm again led her across some sort of a neglected garden.

'Where are you taking me?' she managed to ask.

'You'll see,' he replied gruffly.

Twice she stumbled over the rough ground, and felt the water splash her ankles, but in spite of her protests she was hurried forward, and the grasp on her arm never relaxed. They came eventually to a gate and outside this she saw the dim outline of a car without lights. The shadowy forms of leafless trees towered above her and she heard the moan of the wind in their branches, an eerie sound in the stillness of the night.

Her surroundings told her one thing, however, she was somewhere in the country.

Without releasing his hold the man opened the door of the car, thrust her inside, and climbing in beside her took his place behind the wheel. She heard the whining whirr of the self-starter and the deeper throb of the engine. The machine began to move, swung round, gathered speed and they shot off into the darkness.

Penelope wondered where they were going and what lay at the end of the journey. She tried to see where they were, but the rain blurred the windows of the closed coupé and all she could make out was an indistinct ribbon of passing hedges on either side.

The ride was not a long one. They had barely been travelling for a quarter of an hour before her captor stopped the car and signed to her to get out. She stepped on to a soggy, rutted road and looked about her. Near at hand was the fringe of a thick wood, dark, gloomy and unpleasant looking.

The man caught her by the hand and dragged her under the shelter of the trees.

'Why have you brought me here?' she said.

'Don't ask questions,' he grunted. 'And walk quicker!'

A wave of panic came over her and wrenching her hand free from his grasp she started to run blindly, frantically, back towards the car. The man uttered an oath and swung round.

'Damn you, come here!' he snarled, but with her heart beating wildly she tore forward running as she had never run before in her life — running from the fear that awaited her in the darkness of the wood.

She heard his heavy breathing as he panted along behind her and then she tripped over the root of a tree, stumbled, and fell to her knees. The next second he had gripped her shoulder and dragged her to her feet.

'Got you!' he panted triumphantly. 'Thought you'd get away, did you? You little fool!'

She was too dazed and breathless to answer but her heart sank. Her bid for freedom had failed.

Half dragging and half carrying her he went forward again. Presently they came to a little clearing and in front she saw to her surprise, the dim outline of a small building. It was little more than a hut and appeared to be built of stone. The man with her approached a narrow door and pulled a key from his pocket. Thrusting it into the lock he turned it and kicked the door open with his foot. He dragged her inside and flung her from him.

'You stay there,' he growled. 'The Boss'll see you presently.'

He went out, slamming and locking the door behind him.

Left alone in the pitch darkness of her tiny prison house Penelope almost broke down. The control she had kept over herself was wearing thin and she had an insane desire to scream and shout and beat at the walls. It was only by a tremendous effort that she forced herself to be calm.

Stumbling about in the darkness she presently found a chair and sat down. Who was the Boss the man had mentioned? If he was the person she believed him to be she could expect no mercy. She would have given a lot for a cigarette, but the little case was in her handbag and what had happened to that she had no idea.

The darkness round her was so intense that it was almost a palpable thing. The only sound that broke the oppressive stillness was an irregular tap-tapity-tap on the roof, which she guessed was caused by the rain dripping from the overshadowing trees.

How long it was before the other sound reached her ears she was unable to tell — it seemed an age, but it could not have been very long — the soft sound of an approaching footstep outside. Unconsciously as she heard it she clenched her hands and waited, every muscle and nerve taut while those approaching steps drew nearer and nearer. They stopped outside the door and she heard the rattle of a key in the lock. Straining her eyes to see through the darkness she felt a wave of increasing terror sweep over her.

She could see nothing, but a cool wind told her that the door was opening.

'Are you there, Marion Hayford?' said a soft voice, and at the sound the muscles of her throat loosened and she screamed.

# 19

## A Remembered Voice

'Stop that noise!' snapped the newcomer, and her momentary panic abated.

She had by no means lost her fear, but she realised the futility of giving way to it. Clenching her teeth tightly she crouched back in her chair, keeping her eyes fixed on the place from which the voice had come.

'That's right. Keep calm,' it said. 'It will be much better for you if you do.'

'What do you want? Who are you?' she gasped with dry lips.

'Never mind who I am,' was the reply. 'That doesn't concern you in the least.'

'You're Clark Quinton!' she accused. 'I recognised your voice the moment you spoke.'

'If you knew that why did you ask?' he said coolly. 'You're quite right, I am Clark Quinton.'

She had expected it, but the confirmation of her expectations sent a shiver of fear through her.

'What do you want with me?' she asked as steadily as she could.

'Your intelligence should tell you,' he retorted. 'You are the only menace to my safety. If you'd left well alone and refrained from poking your nose where it wasn't wanted you wouldn't be in the position you are. You and the man working for you found out too much.'

So he knew of the man in Viddle Street. She had not expected *that*.

'What do you intend to do with me?' she said, though her instinct told her the answer.

'There is only one thing to do with people who know too much,' said the voice softly. 'And that is to make sure they cannot pass on that knowledge.'

'Mr. Annerly knows all that I know,' she said.

He gave a soft chuckle.

'He *knew* all that you know,' he corrected, and she understood the significance of the tense.

'You mean that — that — ' she stopped.

'He has been dealt with,' Quinton broke in. 'Did you suppose that I should make the mistake of leaving either of you in a position to talk of what you knew?'

She was silent. There was nothing she could say, and to argue would be useless. She knew sufficient of this man who stood in the darkness before her to realise that any appeal to his better nature would be a waste of breath. Not that she had the slightest intention of making such an appeal, even if it had had the remotest possibility of saving her. There was a streak of pride in her nature which rose up against the mere thought. It was this same pride which had prevented her mentioning the name of Clark Quinton when she had stood in the dock in an American Court of Justice.

The soft voice broke in on her thoughts.

'It is a great pity,' said Quinton 'that you should have driven me to this extreme. Even now, if you care to throw in your lot with me it is not too late.'

'I'd sooner die!' she flashed.

'I'm afraid that's the alternative,' he answered. 'You're a very foolish girl, Marion, but you always were. I'm going to leave you now, but if you've any idea in your head that you may be able to escape you can forget it. This place is built of stone and the door is new, four inches thick and made of solid oak. I had it specially fitted in readiness for your arrival. In all but appearance it is similar to a prison cell, so you ought to feel at home.'

He gave another hateful chuckle and she heard the door close with a thud. He locked it and his footsteps faded away in the distance.

She breathed a sigh of relief. The strain of that interview had been almost unbearable, and she preferred the lonely darkness to his company. And yet once —

Well, that was all over and done with. She had achieved her object. After a patient search she had found Clark Quinton, but she had found him in circumstances which she had not expected. All her plans and schemes had crumbled, and the project which had brought her to England had ended in disaster.

The tears came to her eyes in spite of all her efforts to stop them, and trickled slowly down her cheeks. She had tried so hard and she had been so near to success.

Curiously enough the thought of what her own fate might be didn't trouble her. She knew that this was the end, but how her death would be encompassed worried her very little. If she was to die, she would die, and that was that. The immediate prospect of spending hours in her unpleasant surroundings seemed of greater importance. If only she had some means of getting a light it would not be so unpleasant . . .

She rose to her feet and began to feel her way about the place. She came to a table, a rough table, that her sense of touch told her was of the kind generally found in rustic summerhouses. Slowly with outstretched hands she moved forward until her fingers came in contact with the cold, bare, stone of a wall. Keeping contact with this she moved slowly round the little hut. It was not very big, apparently, for she had scarcely gone three yards when she was brought up by another wall at right angles to the one she was following. Half way along this she discovered a mantelpiece and moving her hands over its dusty surface could have cried out with joy as they came in contact with a box of matches. There were only three and she struck one of these carefully.

In the flickering flame she saw that the place was even smaller than she had imagined. The mantelpiece was built round a tiny fireplace and near to where she had discovered the matches was two inches of candle stuck to the stone shelf. She lit the wick, breathing a prayer of thankfulness. For a little while at least she would have light.

When the flame burned up she took stock of the place and decided that it was not very prepossessing. The stone chamber was roughly nine feet square and the entire furniture consisted of two garden chairs and the table. The fireplace was opposite the door and in the adjacent wall was a window, but a thick wooden shutter had been carefully screwed over this, and although she examined the screws she quickly found that without tools it would be impossible to shift them. She looked up the tiny flue, but it was so small that nothing larger than a rabbit could have passed through it.

The light was a relief after that inky darkness, and she calculated that the candle would burn for at least a couple of hours.

She went over and sat down by the table, resting her elbows on it and supporting her chin on her cupped hands. Perhaps after all there was a way out of her predicament. The effects of the drug had almost completely worn off and her brain felt clearer and more able to cope with the situation. In the midst of her thoughts she suddenly discovered that she was ravenously hungry and wondered whether it was the intention of Clark Quinton to starve her to death.

She considered the possibility quite calmly and was surprised at herself. The fear she had felt had completely left her, and she accounted for this by the fact that she was no longer facing the unknown. She knew now what lay in store for her, at least, she knew to a certain extent, and decided that this was the reason she was so calm. Fear and terror are the outcomes of mystery. It is the fear of what may be lurking in the shadows that makes a child afraid of the dark.

Her hunger was getting unbearable, and in order to take her mind off it she went over to the door and examined the lock. It was a new one and without the key unopenable. She would have liked to have known the time, but a glance at the little watch on her wrist showed her that it had stopped at ten minutes to ten. How long ago was it since she had left the Park Hotel to keep her appointment with Fay Langley? Was it still the same day, or another? She had no means of telling, and then she remembered something. It had been Thursday when she had gone to tea with the girl. If this was Friday Arnold Lake would be calling at the hotel to keep his appointment with her for lunch. He would discover her absence and learn that she had not returned since the previous day. And he was a detective!

Hope filled her heart. Would he guess that her absence was not of her own causing? He knew of the attempt to chloroform her in the taxi. Surely he would realise that this was a more successful extension of that attempt.

She went back to the table and sat down. He was bound to. It must be the first thing that would suggest itself to him. But even supposing it did how was he going to trace her in time? She did not see how he could possibly find her. There was nothing to show him where she had been taken to. Nothing even to connect her with the flat in Kensington.

Alternately hopeful and despairing she sat motionless, staring before her, and then slowly her head began to droop, and as tired nature asserted itself and she fell asleep the candle on the mantelpiece burned down, flickered, went out, and plunged the room once more in darkness.

# 20

## The Man Called Gore

Arnold Lake stared down at the dead man, his lips compressed. There was no doubt that it was a case of murder. The position of the knife told him that.

He had been aware, coming up the stairs, of a peculiar acrid smell, and now he placed the cause of it. It was the smell of burnt cordite. Dropping to his knees he sniffed the barrel of the automatic clenched so tightly in the dead man's hand. It had been recently fired, and as a further confirmation of this fact he found, near the body, the ejected shell. The man had seen his murderer, had fired and missed, and before he could fire again had received the vicious thrust from that ugly-looking knife which had brought about his death.

Arnold rose to his feet and let his eyes rove round the dingy apartment. The furniture was meagre, the floor bare of carpet. The bed consisted of a few blankets and a rug which had been hastily thrown aside as though the man had been lying down when he had heard some sound which had aroused his suspicion. The young inspector noticed that he was minus his boots.

He made a quick search of the room after raising the blind to admit the daylight, but he found nothing of any importance. In a cupboard he discovered a bottle of ink, a pen, and a pad of paper, beside which were half a dozen blank envelopes. But there was no sign of clothing or anything in the nature of pyjamas. It was fairly obvious that the man on the floor had not lived in the place but had only used it as a kind of headquarters. For what object?

Arnold was puzzled. He was less puzzled to account for the man's death. The motive for that was contained in the letter which he had found in Penelope's room at the Park Hotel. This man Barney Gore had discovered something against somebody and that somebody had insured his silence.

There was a bullet hole through one of the panels of the door and a mark on the wall of the passage beyond. Taking out his penknife Arnold probed the plaster and presently found what he sought. A little, misshapen, conical blob of metal, a nickel-cased bullet, obviously fired from an automatic.

Leaving the room of death with its grim occupant he made a hasty search through the house. But the other rooms were empty and contained not even a chair to form any semblance of furnishing. He came to the hall and let himself gently out the front door. Several of the inhabitants of Viddle Street were still gossiping to each other, and he saw their stares of astonishment as he emerged from number ten and walked swiftly up the street.

Meadow Lane was not very far away, and in less than ten minutes after leaving Viddle Street he was talking to the inspector of 'M' division. That stolid man listened to what he had to say, put several questions, and sent for his sergeant.

'Get on to the Divisional Surgeon and ask him to come here as soon as possible,' he ordered. 'Tell him it's a case of murder.'

While he was issuing his instructions Arnold got through to Scotland Yard. He was put in touch with the Area Superintendent, and briefly related his discovery.

'I think it's connected with the gang who did the Westland Bank job and the raid on Cranleigh's, sir,' he said when he had explained.

'Chief-Inspector Chedley's in charge of that business,' said the Superintendent curtly. 'All right, Inspector, I'll arrange for a police tender to be at Viddle Street as soon as possible.'

Arnold hung up the receiver and discovered that the Divisional Inspector was waiting for him. As they were leaving the station house he remembered something.

'You'd better bring some means of opening the door,' he said. 'I had to shut it and there's no way of getting in.'

The inspector nodded, and going back to his office returned with a bunch of skeleton keys.

'We took these off a chap who was pulled in last night,' he said. 'They ought to do the trick. You wait for the doctor,' he added to the sergeant, 'and bring him along with you directly he comes.'

He set off with Arnold accompanied by a constable. They arrived at number ten to the intense excitement of the denizens of the street who were still standing at their open doorways.

It took the inspector some time to open the front door, but he succeeded eventually, and they entered the narrow, dark passage. Leaving the constable below on guard they ascended the stairs and Arnold led the way to the room of death. Everything was just as he had left it, and as he pointed out the various items of interest the Divisional Inspector grunted.

'Seems funny he shouldn't have lived here,' he muttered. 'Which means he must have lived somewhere else. We'll have to find out where. I wonder what his object was in renting this place?'

This puzzled Arnold, and it must have been even more mysterious to the inspector, for he knew nothing about the letter which Lake had discovered in Penelope's room at the Park Hotel.

'How did you come to make this

discovery?' asked the inspector suddenly, and Arnold, who had been dreading the question, hesitated.

'I made the discovery in connection with a clue I was following up concerning another case,' he answered, after a pause. 'I believe that this man had in his possession vital information and I called to see him, but could get no reply to my knocking. I went round to examine the back and discovered a window open and entered the house.'

The inspector pursed his lips in a silent whistle.

'You took a risk,' he said. 'If the man had been alive he might have made it very unpleasant for you.'

'I'm aware of that,' said Arnold. 'But I took the risk, and it was lucky I did.'

They heard the sound of voices in the hall and the Divisional Inspector went to the head of the stairs.

'Who's that, Gibbs?' he called sharply.

'Doctor Makins, sir,' answered the constable.

'Come up, Doctor,' said the inspector. 'I'm glad you've arrived, we were waiting for you.'

The Divisional Surgeon was a short, thin man, who looked as if he carried the worries of the world on his shoulders. His forehead was wrinkled in a perpetual frown and the corners of his thin mouth drooped pathetically.

'Murder, is it?' he asked in a reedy voice that was a trifle husky.

The Divisional Inspector nodded.

'I think so,' he answered. 'You'll be able to tell us more about that.'

Doctor Makins looked at the body and searching in his pocket took out a metal spectacle case. With great care he adjusted a pair of steel-rimmed spectacles on the bridge of his thin nose, returned the case to his pocket and knelt down beside the man on the floor.

'Murder without a doubt,' he said after a short examination. 'Impossible for him to have inflicted this wound himself. Must have been dead for some days, too. Three, I should say. But I can't be very accurate on that till I've made a post-mortem. The knife was driven with considerable force. The man who killed him must have been pretty strong. It was

246

thrust in an upward direction which is a little unusual.' He peered at the hand holding the automatic and felt the fingers. 'He died with that in his hand,' he said. 'There's no possibility of it having been put there after death.'

When he had finished and moved out of the way the Divisional Inspector conducted a search of the dead man's clothing, piling the contents of the pockets beside him on the floor. There was nothing of much interest and he grunted disappointedly.

'Not very helpful,' he said regarding the small heap dubiously. 'Looks to me as if he's taken particular care to carry nothing about with him by which he could be identified.'

'He was known as Barney Gore,' put in Arnold.

'Which I should think was as far away from his own name as possible,' said the Divisional Inspector. 'This is a curious case, and I suppose you know more about it than I do. What was the information you were hoping to get from him?'

'It was in connection with the disappearance of a lady, a Miss Penelope

Hayes,' answered the young inspector.

The elder man looked at him sharply.

'Penelope Hayes?' he repeated. 'Isn't that the girl who charged 'Cosh' Martin with snatching her handbag?'

'It is,' said Arnold.

'Disappeared, has she?' muttered the Divisional Inspector. 'H'm, she was in trouble the other night wasn't she? Somebody tried to kidnap her and you prevented it. Isn't that right?'

Arnold nodded.

'And you think this man knew something about her disappearance?'

'I don't know whether *he* knew anything about her disappearance or not,' said Arnold carefully, 'but I believe he was in a position to supply a clue to the people responsible.'

'And they killed him before he could talk, eh?' the inspector scratched his chin. 'D'you think they're mixed up with these robberies?'

'I think it's possible,' replied Arnold.

He had no wish to go into details with the Divisional Inspector. When Chedley arrived he would have to tell him all he knew. He was not looking forward to it, for without a doubt it would lead to a reprimand. The conversation he had had with Captain Nansen should, most certainly, have been reported immediately, and the fact that he had failed to do so would not meet with the Chief Inspector's approval.

'You're keeping something back,' said the local man. 'But I won't press you. This job will be out of my hands when the Yard people arrive, though I suppose I shall be saddled with most of the work.'

The Divisional Surgeon who had been standing by polishing his glasses in silence broke in on this conversation.

'Don't want me any more, do you, Grays?' he asked.

Inspector Grays hesitated.

'I think you'd better stop, Makins,' he replied. 'The Yard people may want to see you.'

The thin doctor shrugged his shoulders.

'Well, I hope they hurry up,' he grumbled. 'It's getting near my surgery time.'

They had to wait a quarter of an hour

before they heard the police tender draw up outside the house. Chief-Inspector Chedley was the first up the stairs, and he was followed by a crowd of men. Two of his staff carried a big camera and Arnold recognised two others as experts from the fingerprint department.

Chedley's eyes took a quick survey of the room and then he beckoned to the young inspector.

'Tell me all you know about this,' he said curtly.

'Come into one of the other rooms,' whispered Arnold. 'It'll take a little time, sir.'

Chedley shot him a quick look and went into a small, bare room on the other side of the landing. When he had closed the door Arnold told him the whole story. He listened without comment till the young inspector had finished.

'Curious business,' he remarked. 'This man Nansen was certain about the girl?'

'He said he was positive,' replied Arnold.

'Do you think he can be relied on?' asked the Chief Inspector.

Arnold would have liked to say no, but

in fairness to Nansen he couldn't.

'From what I know of him he's thoroughly reliable,' he replied.

'Friend of Superintendent Glinder, isn't he?' said Chedley thoughtfully, and when Arnold nodded. 'That ought to be good enough. You ought to have reported this before, you know. But we'll go into that later. Let's go back and have a look at this fellow.'

He crossed the landing to the larger room. His men were hanging about waiting for instructions, but in silence he entered, and going over to the body looked down at it.

Arnold saw him start, and saw the expression of his face change.

'What did you say this man called himself?' he enquired curtly.

'Barney Gore, sir,' answered Arnold.

'H'm, well, it wasn't his name,' said Chedley. 'Poor fellow. Poor old Jack!'

'Do you know him?' asked the young inspector in astonishment.

'I knew him,' corrected Chief-Inspector Chedley. 'He used to be Area Superintendent for this District before he retired.'

'Good Lord!' It was Divisional Inspector Grays who uttered the ejaculation. 'You don't mean it's John Annerly, sir?'

Chedley looked at him and nodded.

'It is,' he said quietly.

'I thought there was something familiar about him,' muttered Grays. 'I was a sergeant when he was in charge of this area. That's a long time ago.'

'He's been retired five years,' said Chedley. 'He set up a private enquiry agency and did quite well I believe.' He dropped his eyes to the sprawling figure and shook his head. 'The question is what was he doing living in this slum calling himself Barney Gore?' he said thoughtfully.

# 21

## Mr. Sholter is Nervous

Slipping a large portion of toast and marmalade into his capacious mouth, Mr. Ely Sholter munched stolidly, a frown on his face and a worried expression in his little eyes.

He was seated at breakfast and the multi-hued dressing gown which encased his ample form accentuated the sallowness of his face. One side of his pyjama collar stuck rakishly up against his plump chin, and his bald head glistened in the pale sunlight that came through the windows of his flat.

He gulped a cup of coffee noisily and going over to a box on the sideboard helped himself to a cigar. When he had carefully lighted it he began to pace up and down the dining room, his hands behind his back, his chin sunk on his breast.

He was perturbed, and the cause of his perturbation lay in the instructions which had reached him the previous day from his employer. He had read the numerous typed sheets with an ever-growing sense of uneasiness. The enormity of the scheme had taken his breath away, for in those typed sheets was a detailed plan for the stealing of the three million pounds that was being sent to France on the twenty-seventh.

It was a colossal undertaking, and Mr. Sholter was nervous. It was not that he could find any loophole in the scheme that had been sent to him. That was perfect down to the smallest detail. Everything had been taken into account and allowed for. But he felt that the project was so colossal and its carrying out would entail such an outcry that his nerve failed him at the prospect.

He wished that the unknown would confine his energies to something a little less spectacular. Three million pounds was all very well, a very nice sum of money, but it was infinitely safer to acquire it by degrees than to go after it in one enormous coup.

He had said as much when the 'Clever Fellow' had put through his usual nightly call, but the other had cut his protestations short.

'Nonsense!' he had said. 'It is impossible that our organisation can hope to be successful for ever. The thing is to clean up as much as we can in a short time and finish. If this is successful it will be our final effort. Immediately we have carried it out the men who are working for us can be paid off and you can make arrangements to sell the taxi business. Apart from the unknown side of it, it is a profitable concern and it shouldn't be difficult. You've got your instructions, carry them out!'

Since it was useless arguing, Mr. Sholter had proceeded to carry them out. Already he had issued the orders necessary for the preliminary part of the scheme. But he was distinctly uneasy. Some sixth sense warned him that things were rapidly approaching a crisis. It may have been that the failure of the raid on Cranleigh's had upset him. This had been the first set-back he had experienced, and it had certainly shaken his nerve.

He was troubled, too, about this girl, Penelope Hayes. He had no inkling as to how she came into it or why his employer had been so anxious to get hold of her, and for some reason or other the fact irritated and disturbed him.

There was quite a lot of which he was quite ignorant, and he didn't like being in the dark. He would have preferred to know exactly what was going on, so that if anything went wrong he could take the necessary precautions. It wasn't that he cared twopence what happened to his mysterious employer or any of the men who worked for him, but he was very greatly concerned with the welfare of Ely Sholter, and was averse to anything that might jeopardise it.

He finished his cigar, shaved, bathed and dressed, and, ordering his car, drove down to the garage in Waterloo Road. There was nothing here to add to his nervousness. An interview with Billing revealed that everything was working smoothly. The majority of his instructions had been carried out, and reports concerning these awaited him on his desk. He read them through, made several pencilled notes, and unlocking the safe took out the bulky packet of typewritten instructions and settled down to read them for the twentieth time.

He had reached the last page when the loud-speaking telephone on his desk interrupted him.

'That air fellow's here,' said Billing's voice. 'Shall I send him into you?'

Mr. Sholter reached out his hand and turned a switch.

'In five minutes,' he said.

Rising to his feet he collected the typewritten sheets which he had been reading and going over to the safe carefully locked them away. Returning to his desk he searched among the papers on it until he found the one he sought. For some little while he studied this, nodding to himself, and then, laying it down waited for the arrival of his visitor.

The man whom Billing showed into the office a few moments later was of sufficiently striking appearance to have called for a second glance even in a crowd. He was tall, and the leanness of his body was the leanness of the athlete. Although obviously not an old man, his hair was so grey that it was almost silver, and the face beneath was lined with care and worry.

'Good morning, Captain Rawlton,' greeted Mr. Sholter pleasantly.

'Mr. Rawlton,' corrected the newcomer harshly, and there was a sneer of bitterness on his thin lips. 'I was only a temporary gentleman!'

'Mister, then, if you prefer it,' said Mr. Sholter. 'Sit down, will you?'

He indicated a chair in front of his desk and Rawlton dropped into it. Billing had withdrawn after announcing him, and Mr. Sholter went over and locked the door.

'Now,' he said coming back to the desk, 'we can talk without interruption.' He pushed a box of cigars over to his visitor and with a slight raising of his eyebrows the other took one.

'What is it you want with me?' he asked. 'I was told by a resident of the common lodging house in which I live that there might be a job going if I came to see you. Is that right?'

'Partly right,' said Mr. Sholter. 'You are, I believe, an expert air pilot?'

Rawlton shrugged his shoulders.

'I was,' he said. 'But I haven't handled a plane now for some time.'

'Not since you came out of prison,' said Mr. Sholter gently, and the other's eyes narrowed.

'Oh, you know that, do you,' he grunted.

'I know quite a lot,' said the stout man. 'I know that your sentence of nine months would have been considerably extended if the police had known about the other little business.'

With an oath Rawlton sprang to his feet.

'What do you mean?' he said thickly. 'What are you getting at?'

'Sit down, Mr. Rawlton, sit down,' said Mr. Sholter smoothly. 'There is nothing to get excited about. You know very well what I mean. I am referring to the money that was missing from the cashier's office at the aerodrome at which you were employed, prior to your second lapse.'

The lean face of the man before him hardened.

'So you know about that, do you,' he muttered. 'What is this, a police trap?'

'Certainly not, my dear sir,' said Mr. Sholter. 'But it is just as well to make things quite clear before I put forward my proposal.'

Rawlton's eyes were suspicious as he slowly sat down again.

'You took two hundred and fifty pounds from the cashiers' department at Radley Aerodrome,' said Mr. Sholter pleasantly, 'and you were never suspected because a mechanic who had been guilty of petty pilfering was charged with the crime and suffered in your stead. Later you were arrested for passing useless cheques, and for that you received a sentence of nine months. Since then you have been practically down and out. No, wait, I haven't finished yet,' as Rawlton opened his lips. 'I'm not blaming you. Your war record is excellent, and those who fought in that great catastrophe were not treated any too generously after it was over.'

'By heaven you're right!' muttered Rawlton.

'No doubt,' continued Mr. Sholter, 'you were exposed to great temptation, and, being merely human, you fell. Now, I am prepared to put a proposition to you, which, if you are willing to undertake it will put five thousand pounds in your pocket.'

Rawlton stared at him.

'Are you crazy or am I?' he demanded. 'What can I do that is worth five thousand pounds to you?'

'That I will tell you in a moment,' said Mr. Sholter. 'There are certain conditions attaching to my offer which I feel you ought to hear before we go into the details. The mechanic I mentioned is still serving a sentence for the theft of the money you stole. Should information reach the police concerning the person really responsible they will not hesitate to act immediately.' His stubby hands reached out and he tapped the paper he had been reading prior to the arrival of his visitor. 'I may add that I have full particulars here,' he went on. 'And in the event of your not accepting my offer I shall feel it my duty, as a respectable citizen, to forward this document to Scotland Yard.'

Rawlton's lips curled.

'That sounds to me as if I had no choice,' he remarked slowly. 'In other words, I do as you want me to, or you'll have me arrested. Is that it?'

'I should scarcely have put it so crudely,' said Mr. Sholter. 'But that is, shall we say, something like it.'

'H'm, well, put forward your proposition,' said the other curtly. 'And I don't mind telling you there isn't much I wouldn't do for five thousand pounds.'

'That's the sort of talk I like to hear,' said Mr. Sholter rubbing his hands briskly. 'Now, listen, Mr. Rawlton.'

He pulled his chair close up to the desk and began to speak rapidly. At his first words Rawlton sat up with a start and his wonder and interest increased as the stout man continued. When he had finished there was a long silence, broken at last by Mr. Sholter.

'Well, what d'you say?' he asked. 'There's fifty per cent on account and the balance when you've completed the job.'

'Produce your two thousand five hundred!' said Rawlton. 'I'll do it! For five thousand pounds I'd go to hell and through!'

# 22

George Seeper Disappears.

Annerley's Private Enquiry Agency occupied a small suite of offices in Chancery Lane. Suite is, perhaps, a slightly exaggerated term to apply to the two rooms on the third floor which constituted the working quarters of the firm, for one large room had been divided by a piece of beaver-board partition to form an outer and inner office. The single elderly clerk who formed the entire staff of Annerley's was preparing to leave for the day when Arnold Lake and Chief-Inspector Chedley arrived on the scene.

After Chedley's astonishing identification of the dead man in Viddle Street, the Chief-Inspector had looked up the address of the offices and decided to pay a visit without further delay. It was not that he had any doubt that the man who had posed as Barney Gore was John

Annerly, but he hoped that a visit to the ex-detective's business would result in some information that would give him a lead to his murderer.

The grey-haired clerk, whose name was Tindal, was horrified at the news.

'Dead . . . Murdered . . . Mr. Annerly?' he gasped incredulously. 'How did it happen, sir?'

Chedley explained briefly.

'D'you know why he was living at Viddle Street under the name of Barney Gore?' he concluded.

The clerk shook his head dumbly. It was obvious that he had received a great shock.

'No, sir,' he said slowly. 'I can't tell you that. I know Mr. Annerly was very busy on a case. Something to do with a young lady who called here several times, but what it was all about I don't know. Mr. Annerly was like that, sir, he didn't tell me much.'

'He wouldn't,' said Chedley. 'When he was at the Yard he exasperated everybody by that habit of reticence. He liked to keep everything to himself until he'd got the job worked out to the last detail, and then he'd spring his surprise. This young lady you're talking about, what was she like?'

The clerk essayed a description, and although it was a very bad one Arnold had no difficulty in recognising Penelope.

'Is that the girl you were talking about?' asked Chedley, and he nodded.

'Perhaps there's something in his office,' grunted the Chief-Inspector, 'that'll tell us a bit more.'

He consulted with the still dazed clerk, and the latter produced keys. The door of the inner room was unlocked and they were shown into a bare, neat office which was a trifle larger than the outer one. Evidently the late John Annerly had not gone in much for comfort, or more probably his long service in the Metro-politan Police Force had reconciled him to working amid surroundings in which only the bare necessities for labour were used. His private sanctum was austere in the extreme. A large plain wooden desk occupied the centre of the linoleum-covered floor. Behind this was a swivel chair, and on a worn rug in front a shabby armchair. A small safe occupied one corner and opposite to it was a built-in cupboard. A low bookcase containing a few reference books completed the meagre furnishing.

The top of the desk was devoid of papers. A writing pad, an ink stand, a perpetual calendar and the telephone were the only things ranged neatly on its inkstained top.

Chedley glanced about him and turned to the clerk who was hovering round them.

'Have you got the key to that safe?' he asked.

The elderly man shook his head.

'No, sir,' he answered. 'Mr. Annerly always kept that.'

The Chief-Inspector went across to it and tried the door. As he had expected, it was locked. He turned his attention to the built-in cupboard. This was unlocked, but a glance in the interior showed him that it contained nothing of importance. The shelves were stacked neatly with stationary and several spare files, new and empty. Closing the door he came over to the desk and tried the drawers. With the exception of one they were unlocked and with Arnold's help Chedley rapidly went through them.

There was nothing helpful, and fingering his chin the Chief-Inspector stared at the locked centre drawer.

'We didn't find any keys on the body,' he said, 'so either the murderer took them away with him or they're elsewhere. I wonder if one of mine will fit this lock?'

He took a bunch of keys from his pocket and tried. At the fifth attempt he succeeded, and pulled open the narrow receptacle. In it was a private letter file, a number of receipted bills and a small red covered notebook. Chedley pounced on the letter file and the notebook and seating himself in the desk chair began to examine them.

'Here's a letter from the girl,' he said, 'making an appointment.' And showed his find to Arnold.

It was dated five months previously and had evidently been the first letter she had written to Annerly. She mentioned that she wished him to undertake some important business for her, but the nature of the business was not revealed. There were no other letters from her in the file and Chedley turned his attention to the notebook.

Here they discovered several references to Penelope Hayes. Annerly had contracted her name to the initials, P.H. On one page was a reference to Clark Quinton, and Chedley looked at Arnold.

'That's the name of the man she mentioned to you, isn't it?' he asked.

'That's the man,' said the young inspector. 'She said he was the worst man in the world.'

'From these notes,' grunted Chedley, 'it looks as though she had commissioned Annerly to find him. Listen to this.' He read a passage from the book. ''A man answering the description of C.Q. appears to have been seen in the Deptford district. Write P.H. and arrange to take her to the place where he usually goes for identification.' That's the man we want,' said Chedley. 'Clark Quinton. I don't think there's much doubt that he's the fellow who killed poor Annerly. Now, why was the girl so keen on finding him?'

Arnold had no suggestion to offer. The discovery of the murdered ex-detective had, for the moment, distracted his mind from the girl's peril, but now the fear he had experienced when he had learned of her disappearance came back with redoubled force.

Chedley, who was watching him, saw the change in his face and guessed the cause.

'I know what you're thinking, son,' he said kindly. 'That this man has also got the girl. I think you're right. What it was she knew about him I don't know, and why she was so anxious to find him I don't know, but I guess the reason he killed Annerly and the reason this girl has vanished is because they both knew too much for his safety. She called him the worst man in the world, didn't she? Well, that may be an exaggeration, but I should say she was pretty nearly right!' He rose to his feet, closed the notebook and picked it up, together with the letter file. 'I'll take these with me,' he said to the clerk. 'Now, what was Mr. Annerly's private address?'

Tindal gave it to him — Sixteen Cromer Road, Clapham Junction — and Chedley noted it down.

When they had made a search of the outer office, and with the assistance of the clerk had consulted all the files and found nothing further to help them, they took their departure, having ascertained where to get hold of Tindal in case of emergency.

'Our next call is Cromer Road,' said Chedley as they climbed into the 'Q' car. 'Perhaps we can pick up something there.'

He was silent and thoughtful as they sped in the direction of Clapham Junction and Arnold was grateful, for his own thoughts were fully occupied in worrying over the girl.

Cromer Road was one of those long, straight, roads, lined on either side by small houses, all exactly alike. Number sixteen's only difference to its fellows lay in the colour of the window curtains which were a pale shade of green. Chedley noticed it as he got out of the car and grunted.

'Annerly's favourite colour,' he muttered.

A small, thin-visaged woman opened the door in answer to his ring and eyed him enquiringly. Chedley explained who he was and the object of his visit, and if the housekeeper, for this she turned out to be, felt any emotion at the news of her employer's tragic death she gave no outward sign of it. Her small eyes fixed the Chief-Inspector with a bird-like stare as he told her the circumstances, and the expression of her face remained unaltered except for a slight tightening of her thin lips. Quite calmly she gave them every assistance in searching the house.

Chedley's optimism was not justified. There was nothing here that threw any light on the reason for the ex-detective's violent death. In his bedroom they did find a bunch of keys, however, one of which was obviously the key of the safe, and with these in his possession Chedley drove back again to Chancery Lane.

Tindal, the clerk, had gone, but they had secured from him a duplicate key of the office and admitted themselves. But

272

once again they drew a blank. The safe contained several ledgers and cash accounts but nothing concerning John Annerly's business so far as related to the work he was engaged in. Penelope Hayes had evidently paid a heavy retaining fee, for they found an item in the ledger against her initials showing that she had paid him two hundred pounds shortly after the date of the letter making her first appointment, and another item — a more recent one — showing a similar sum.

'I suppose he kept all his business in his head,' muttered Chedley, making no effort to conceal his disappointment. 'He always hated committing things to writing, which is a great pity as far as we are concerned.'

He sighed wearily and looked round the gloomy office.

'Well, there's nothing more we can do at the moment,' he went on, 'except go back to the Yard and have an 'all stations' call sent out with a description of the girl and a request for any information concerning Clark Quinton.'

Arnold gathered from the tone of his

voice that he didn't expect much from this routine enquiry.

It was half past nine when they reached the Yard, and Arnold was nearly dead from worry and weariness. He reported to Superintendent Glinder and set off to walk the short distance to his flat, his mind in a chaotic state of doubts and fears. He could do nothing, and yet he felt that he was wasting time, that while he was inactive Penelope was facing the gravest possible danger.

He no longer tried to disguise from himself his feelings for the girl. In some mysterious way she had, from the first, become a large part of his life, and although he had only seen her two or three times he knew that without her, existence would have no further meaning. The practical side of his nature told him that it was ridiculous that someone who was almost a stranger could have such an effect. But the practical side fought a losing battle. He knew it was ridiculous but at the same time he was completely unable to alter the fact that it was true. She might or might not be a criminal, that made no difference at all. He was in love with her and was quite prepared to sacrifice his career for her sake. Although Chedley had said nothing further about his holding up the information he had got from Nansen, Arnold knew that he would hear a great deal more about it; that for the first time since he had joined the police force his sheet would be marred by a severe reprimand.

He was so tired by the time he reached his flat that he was incapable of further coherent thought.

As he wearily climbed the stairs he decided to have a hot bath and go straight to bed. Letting himself in to the little hall he called to George Seeper. There was no reply.

With a muttered imprecation Arnold switched on the light and entered the servant's bedroom, expecting to find him asleep, but the room was unoccupied.

He made a rapid tour of the flat but there was no sign of Seeper.

Concluding the man had gone out, Arnold turned on his bath and proceeded to undress. By the time he had finished and run the water away it was after ten. Clad in pyjamas and a dressing gown he made himself some coffee and waited impatiently for his servant to return.

He must have fallen asleep in his chair for when he awoke, shivering with cold, he discovered to his dismay that it was three o'clock.

'Seeper, confound it! Where are you?' he called, staggering to his feet, still dazed with sleep.

But nobody answered him, because there was nobody there to answer him. George Seeper had not returned!

# 23

## Mr. Seeper Meets With Adventure

Mr. George Seeper was supposed to have one afternoon off each week, and the day on which this usually fell was a Friday. He was a great lover of the more melodramatic type of talking picture and usually spent these leisure hours occupying a seat in his favourite cinema. On this particular Friday afternoon, having arrayed himself like Solomon in all his glory and made his way to his favourite place of entertainment, he was disappointed and annoyed to find that no film that appealed to him was in the programme. There were other picture houses that he could have gone to but Mr. Seeper was conservative in his tastes and preferred to patronise one particular place of entertainment. If they could not provide him with the class of entertainment his soul craved for, then he decided to seek some other means of amusement.

After a certain amount of time spent in cogitation he made up his mind to take a walk. He was fond of a quiet stroll occasionally and not averse to any amorous adventure that a benificent providence might chance to throw in his way. There was something of the Lothario in Mr. Seeper and he had pleasant recollections of past conquests. He had others less pleasant, but philisophically refused to remember these.

He climbed on to a bus and was eventually set down at Marble Arch. Crossing the broad roadway at this point he entered Hyde Park and made his leisurely way towards Rotten Row, his eyes alert for such feminine loveliness as might attract his fancy.

The afternoon was fine, if a little cold, and Mr. Seeper breathed the keen air with enjoyment. There were the usual number of people parading in the Row, including a fair sprinkling of unaccompanied young women, but none of them appealed to Mr. Seeper as being worth the trouble involved in making an acquaintance.

Presently he turned off into a side path and struck across the park in a northerly direction. There was a broad walk further on which had, on previous occasions, served him well in his quest for promiscuous companionship.

He was halfway along the path which led to this when he saw two men approaching. He eyed them incuriously as they drew nearer, and then as they passed him he heard the smaller one say to the other: 'Gave that busy fellow Lake a shock . . . ' 'Sweet on that girl . . . '

Mr. Seeper heard no more, but what he had heard gave his mind a considerable jerk, for as he very well knew, 'busy fellow' was the London thief's argot for 'detective,' and 'Lake' could only refer to his employer. He had no idea what they meant by the reference to 'that girl,' for he had as yet heard nothing about the disappearance of Penelope Hayes. But his quick brain told him that these men were in some way connected with the attempt on his master's life in Shardilloes Road.

His eyes narrowed. Here was a bit of luck. If he followed these two until he came across a policeman he could hand them over to the charge of the law and receive the grateful thanks of Arnold Lake when he returned to the flat.

He slowed in his walk, and turning, began to follow cautiously in their wake. They were neither of them very prepossessing individuals; shabbily dressed and typical of the lower class of crook. Mr. Seeper, who was well acquainted with this genus, placed them pretty quickly. They were 'toughs' willing to undertake anything and everything that would bring them sufficient money to back their fancies at the 'Dogs' and dull what few senses they possessed with drink.

They were making for the Marble Arch entrance, and Mr. Seeper, spotting a policeman on the opposite side of the road, was in the act of signalling to the man, when a fresh idea occurred to him. If the two men were connected with the bombing of Arnold Lake's car they must also be connected with the mysterious individual whose advent into crime was causing so much trouble to the denizens of Scotland Yard. What a personal triumph it would be for Mr. Seeper if he, alone and unaided, could find this person. He saw himself walking into Scotland Yard and coolly informing the Chief of Police that he had got the man for whom every policeman in the force was looking. It would be a great moment, and appealed to Mr. Seeper's sense of the dramatic.

He stopped his half-hearted signalling to the constable — luckily the man had not been looking in his direction — and continued to trail his quarry.

They went over to the Tube Station and Mr. Seeper was close enough behind them to hear one of them ask the booking clerk for two tickets to Charing Cross. He bought one for the same destination and followed the two men into the lift. They were, apparently, completely unsuspicious that they were being followed, for although they glanced at Mr. Seeper as he passed them they took no further notice of him, and continued to talk in low tones. He caught a word here and there, and discovered that they were discussing the relative merits of two dogs that were running at the White City on the following day.

At Charing Cross they alighted and made their way in to the station. They made for the booking hall, and this time Mr. Seeper was too far behind to hear where they booked to. His cunning wits, however, did not desert him. Waiting until they had passed out of sight he hurried up to the window.

'Two friends of mine have just taken a ticket,' he said, pretending to be breathless. 'I missed them. Give me one too, will you?'

The station official pushed forward a third single to Farnborough. Mr. Seeper tendered a ten shilling note, received his change and with both ticket and change clutched in his hand made his way towards the platform from which the train was due to depart. As he passed the barrier he saw the two men he was trailing getting into a third class compartment near the front. He got in the next one, and lighting a cigarette settled himself complacently back in the corner.

So far so good. He had nothing to do now but wait patiently until the train arrived at Farnborough and follow the men when they left the station. He would have to be a little more careful there, for there would be less people about, and there was a risk that they might recognise him as the man who had got in the lift with them at Marble Arch Tube Station.

The train drew out, and at every stop on the journey Mr. Seeper covertly eyed the platform in case his quarry should leave at an intervening point. He didn't expect them to, but there was just a chance that they might. His fears were groundless, however, for they made no move until the train pulled up at Farnborough, when they got out, and Mr. Seeper followed at a respectful distance.

They passed quickly through the station and went off down the street. Apparently they had no suspicion that they were being trailed, for neither of them once glanced back.

Presently they turned off into a narrow lane, and traversing this came eventually to a tumbledown gate that appeared to Mr. Seeper to give admission to a small farm. Through this they passed, and Mr. Seeper dodged behind the friendly trunk of a massive oak as they gave a glance back along the way they had come.

Allowing a little time to elapse he presently emerged from his hiding place and strolled cautiously past the gate through which they had gone. It gave admittance to a square yard in which some chickens were pecking industriously. Beyond was a low house with whitewashed walls and a thatched roof. Having noticed this much in the hasty glance he gave as he passed the gates Mr. Seeper continued on his way.

The lane was lined by high hedges, and a few yards farther along he came upon a gap in one of these, beyond which lay a meadow that stretched at the back of the little farmlike building. Mr. Seeper cautiously crawled through the gap and found himself ankle deep in rank weeds. A dilapidated fence separated the field from an orchard, and towards this he made his way. At a place where two of the slats had fallen inwards he looked through and was able to see, past the straggling fruit trees, the back of the cottage. It looked rather desolate and uncared for. The outbuildings were half tumbling down and the whole house was in a bad state of repair.

He was in somewhat of a quandary. Although it was growing dusk it was far too light as yet for him to risk going nearer to the house, and while he lurked about the back the two men he had followed might quite easily leave by the front. He rapidly surveyed the situation and decided on a plan of campaign.

Going back to the gap in the hedge he scrambled through into the lane. Almost opposite him was an oak tree and this he proceeded with difficulty to climb. He managed it, however, and presently found himself comfortably ensconced in the fork of two branches, and in a position from which he was able to survey, not only the yard in the front of the cottage, but the back as well.

It was a low, rambling, disreputable building; the yard littered with straw and rotting wood. Although at one time it appeared to have been a small farm, the hen coops were falling to pieces and the whole place gave the appearance of having been neglected for some time.

As the dusk deepened Mr. Seeper began to feel cold. A chilly wind had sprung up and found its way beneath his thin overcoat, causing him to shiver uncomfortably. He was hungry, too, but neither of these things affected his purpose. He had got so far and he was going through with it. Immediately it was dark enough for him to move without risk of his being observed he intended to make a closer inspection of the dilapidated poultry farm, and discover, if possible, what was going on inside.

It seemed an age before it became really dark, and he was shivering from cold and numbed from his cramped position before he eventually decided that he might leave his observation post. Scrambling from the tree he passed through the hole in the hedge and coming to the tumbledown fencing wriggled his way through the broken slats. He was now in the orchard, and began to make his way cautiously towards the rear of the cottage.

There was a light in one of the lower back rooms which shone through a chink in the curtain which had been drawn across the window. Mr. Seeper made for this, and crouching by the sill listened. The low rumble of voices came to his ears but he could hear nothing of what was being said. He tried to see into the room beyond, but the curtains had been pinned across, the chink from which the light shone being high up near the top of the window.

A woman's voice reached him, and he saw her shadow as she passed between the light. He heard the chinking of plates and the clink of glasses, and guessed that some kind of a meal was in progress or being prepared.

Mr. Seeper licked his lips. His hunger was increasing with every passing moment, and in spite of his excitement he could not forget it.

If only he could see into that room. The shadow of the woman passed again in front of the window and was followed by the silhouette of a man struggling into an overcoat.

Mr. Seeper became alert. One of the inhabitants was evidently going out.

A few minutes later he had confirmation of this, for a door banged round at the front, and he heard the crunching of steps crossing the square yard. The back of the house was connected with the front by a narrow alleyway that ran parallel to the hedge bordering the lane, and cautiously he slunk along this, keeping a watchful eye on the gate. The person who had come out, however, had gone in the other direction. Mr. Seeper could still hear him, but he could not see him. It was too dark for that.

He followed in the wake of the retreating footsteps, however, avoiding the rubbish that strewed his path. He heard the click of a gate and presently the noise of a motor engine being started. With his heart beating faster he increased his pace. The person who had left the cottage was evidently going to travel by car somewhere.

Suddenly, almost before he was aware of it he came upon the gate, and beyond caught the red glow of a tail lamp. Opening the gate carefully and noiselessly he found himself in another lane that stretched at right angles to the first, and was sheltered at this point by a thick coppice of trees.

The car was standing a few yards in front of him, and even as he looked it began to move forward, bumping over the rough ground. Mr. Seeper broke into a run. He felt that to lose sight of that car would put an end to any chance of carrying out his highflown ambition. It was a small two-seater with the hood up, and he managed to scramble on the sloping back, wedging one foot on the rear lamp bracket. It was a precarious perch, rendered more so by the rough ground they were traversing, for the car bumped at every foot, and almost jerked him from his none too firm hold.

Presently, however, they came out on to the smoother surface of a secondary road and the going was better. The driver of the coupé increased his speed, and Mr.

Seeper hung on, his heart in his mouth, expecting every second to be thrown into the roadway. Happily the journey was not a long one. All of a sudden the car drew up with a jerk at the fringe of a wood, and Mr. Seeper slid with a sigh of thankfulness to the ground. He was crouching behind a clump of brambles when the door of the car was thrust open and a man got out. It was so dark that he was unable to tell whether this was either of the two men he had followed, but he thought it was the taller of the two.

The country at this point was wild and deserted. The gloomy denseness of the wood looked sinister and unprepossessing. The man took a basket from the car and began to walk swiftly towards the trees. Mr. Seeper went after him, wondering where on earth he was going.

He continued on for some time, and Mr. Seeper followed, dodging from tree trunk to tree trunk, and moving as noiselessly as he could.

Presently the trees thinned to a little clearing, and to his surprise he saw that in the middle of it was a small, stone building. This was obviously the destination of the man from the cottage. Quite suddenly the reason for the basket came to him. The man was carrying food! That was the explanation of the clattering of plates that he had heard while he had been crouching under the window. But who on earth was he taking food to? Who inhabited that small hut of stone?

Mr. Seeper's face was burning with excitement. He felt he was on the verge of making an important discovery. Watching, he saw the man take a key from his pocket and unlock the door. As he disappeared inside and the door clanged to behind him, Mr. Seeper advanced, and his thin lips were set in a determined line. He was going to discover the secret of that hut in the wood or die in the attempt!

# 24

## The Rescue

Penelope awoke shivering with cold and stiff from the uncomfortableness of her position. She opened her eyes in intense darkness, and, still dazed with sleep, reached out her hand to feel for the lamp which she knew should be beside her bed. She was groping about for some time before she realised that she was not in her bed, and memory came flooding back. She was still crouched in the hard chair in which she had fallen asleep. The candle had burnt out and there was no means of getting any more light. Her limbs ached and her mouth and throat were dry.

She eased her position, leaning against the low back of the chair.

She must have slept for some time, for now that she was thoroughly awake she could make out a thin line of greenish-grey light that filtered under the door.

She was ravenously hungry and would have given anything for a cup of really hot, strong tea.

Presently she got up and began to pace up and down in the darkness. The movement warmed her a little, as she hoped it would.

What was going to happen to her? How long did Quinton intend keeping her in this horrible place without light and without food? Was it his intention to starve her to death? He was quite capable of doing such a thing, indeed, it was compatible with everything she knew about him. She shivered. Far better a swift death than that! To be cooped up here until she died from starvation was a dreadful prospect, rendered the more so because of the darkness which surrounded her.

How stupid she had been not to conserve that tiny piece of candle instead of falling to sleep and letting it burn itself out. It would have at least given her a few more moments of blessed light. The strip under the door was growing brighter every second, and she guessed from this that daylight was advancing. It did little, however, to disperse the gloom of her prison.

She paced up and down until she was tired and weary, and then sank once more into her chair. Perhaps Quinton would come back. Even the possibility of another visit from him was welcome. Anything was better than the monotony of this eternal darkness.

She felt the perspiration break out on her forehead, and became aware of an insane desire to throw herself against the door in the hope of breaking out of this awful place.

Realising that she was in danger of becoming hysterical she made a valiant effort and took a grip of her nerves. It was no good letting herself give way. That would do no good. She forced herself to think calmly. Perhaps, after all, Arnold would find her, though how he was going to do so she hadn't the remotest idea. What she must do was to occupy her mind so as to prevent herself from brooding on the unpleasantness of her surroundings.

She began to go over methodically all the incidents of her life, weaving them in the form of a kind of autobiography. She found this effectual, and began to get so interested that she momentarily forgot her hunger and cold.

The day must have become fully advanced, because when she looked again at the streak below the door it was much more vivid, and either her eyes were becoming accustomed to it or the darkness was less intense. Dimly she could make out the table and chair in which she sat, and the walls of her prison house.

She got up again and walked about. She found that she felt better when she was moving. This time she took a different direction and moved round and round the table until the constant circling made her feel dizzy. Once more she wondered what fate Quinton had in store for her, and realised how useless it was conjecturing. Whatever fate had in store for her would happen, and she was powerless to prevent it. The only thing she could do was to meet it as calmly as possible.

The hours dragged slowly by, and from sheer weariness she collapsed in the chair once more, and must have fallen asleep, for she remembered nothing more until she opened her eyes to find that the streak of light under the door had gone and intense blackness enveloping her. She had either slept or been unconscious for a long time. The day had gone and another night had settled down.

She was feeling very weak from lack of food, and her hunger had given place to an unpleasant nausea. She tried to stand up, but an attack of dizziness forced her to remain seated. All sorts of chaotic thoughts filled her brain; little fragments and incidents that followed one another without rhyme or reason. She heard someone singing the chorus of a popular foxtrot and listened, discovering to her surprise that it was herself.

She was becoming lightheaded, and then, like a douche of cold water, she heard the footsteps. Faintly at first and then becoming louder. Quinton was returning. He had come to carry out his threat!

She felt strangely disinterested. In her present state she was very little concerned as to what happened to her.

A key clicked in the lock and a rush of cold air blew on her as the door opened. She heard it shut behind someone, and then a ray of light cut through the darkness as a torch was switched on. She stared at the man who had entered, dimly visible in the reflected light from the electric lamp he carried, and recognised him as the man who had brought her in the first instance to this place. He carried a basket which he set down on the table.

'I've brought you some food,' he grunted surlily. 'I should think you need it. There's some sandwiches, and some coffee in a flask.'

Penelope never remembered having heard such welcome words in her life. With hands that trembled with eagerness she took the big vacuum flask from the basket and filled the screw-cap unsteadily with the hot coffee it contained. Nothing had ever tasted so exquisite as that warm fluid which trickled down her parched throat. She drank greedily.

'You'd better make the most of it,' warned the man watching her. 'You won't get no more till tomorrow night.'

'How long am I going to be kept here?' she asked huskily.

He shrugged his shoulders.

'That's more than I can tell you,' he answered. 'As long as the Guv'nor wants you to be I expect.'

She took one of the thick beef sandwiches and began to eat it ravenously. He watched her in silence until she had finished the last crumb and drained the final drop of coffee.

The food and drink had an almost instantaneous effect. Her brain cleared and the dizziness quickly left her.

He had picked up the basket and was turning towards the door when she stopped him.

'Wait!' she said. 'I've got money. I'll give you a thousand pounds if you'll help me to get away from here.'

'Money ain't no good to a dead man!' he retorted. 'And that's what I'd be twenty-four hours after it was discovered you'd gone.'

'With that amount of money you could get out of the country,' she said quickly.

'Could I!' he laughed harshly. 'I couldn't get out in time. Besides which I'll be getting a fair amount for looking after you.'

'I'll make it two thousand,' she said desperately.

He shook his head.

'You could make it a million, but it wouldn't be no use,' he answered. 'I'd rather be poor and alive than rich and dead.'

The next moment he had gone, shutting and locking the door behind him.

★　★　★

Mr. Seeper saw him depart from the concealment of a clump of trees. With his ear pressed close to the door he had heard enough to assure him that the occupant of the hut was a girl and that she was being kept there against her will. At the first movement the man had made towards the door Mr. Seeper had scuttled, his nimble brain working rapidly to find a plan by which he could become the possessor of the key which would open that stout door. One had suggested itself almost immediately, and as soon as he saw the visitor leave the hut he hurried away in the direction of the waiting car.

Pulling his neat neck-tie loose and tilting his hat at a rakish angle he waited a few yards away up the road until he saw the man reach the machine, and then began to approach him, unsteadily, singing mournfully and very much out of tune, the refrain of one of the latest film theme songs.

He saw the man by the car start and look in his direction, and then as he came nearer he greeted him.

'Shay, ol' feller,' he said thickly, 'where's this road lead to?'

The man by the car eyed him suspiciously.

'If you continue the way you're going,' he said, 'you'll come to St. Mary Cray.'

'Thash where I want to go to,' said Mr. Seeper. 'You goin' that d'rection?'

'No, I'm not!' said the other shortly.

'Pity,' said Mr. Seeper shaking his head. 'Thought you could 'ave given me a lift. S'pose you wouldn't like to give me a lift?' He came a little closer. 'Be a nice friendly action to a poor feller who's been spending the evening with a few pals.'

He swayed, appeared to stumble, and flung his arms round the man by the car to save himself from falling. The man uttered an oath and pushed him off.

'Mind what you're doing, you drunken fool!' he said angrily. 'Look here! You get to hell out of this!'

Mr. Seeper recovered his balance and eyed him gravely.

'No need to be — be abusive,' he said. 'I thought you was a — a pal.'

'You get along,' said the man. 'The quicker you get home the better, I should think.'

'I should think so, too,' said Mr. Seeper. 'But it's going to take me a long time.'

'I don't care if it takes you all night,' said the other impatiently. 'Get out of my way!'

He gave Mr. Seeper a push which sent

that man staggering backwards, climbed into his car and started the engine. As the red tail lamp disappeared down the darkened road Mr. Seeper grinned happily. His hands had not lost their cunning. In that moment when he had embraced the man to save himself from falling he had secured what he wanted, and clutched in the palm of his right hand was the key which opened the door of the hut in the clearing.

# 25

## A Surprise for Arnold

Arnold Lake set about getting himself some breakfast, an irritable and worried man. To add to all his other troubles had come this inexplicable disappearance of George Seeper.

When he had wakened, cold and stiff, in the small hours of that morning and found that his servant was still absent he had not gone to sleep again. Brewing himself some tea he had sat smoking and thinking until the sound of life in the street outside had warned him that the morning was well advanced.

Unless he had met with an accident Arnold could think of no reason for Mr. Seeper's non-return. The man had never absented himself before, and although he searched the little flat thoroughly he could find nothing in the nature of a note explaining his reason for doing so now. It was certainly very annoying, and he determined that when Mr. Seeper *did* return he would give him a piece of his mind.

He ate his breakfast, bathed, shaved and dressed, and went along to Scotland Yard.

Chief-Inspector Chedley had just arrived when he reached the grim building and Arnold reported the absence of his servant. Chedley was not particularly interested.

'Perhaps he got drunk,' he suggested.

But Arnold shook his head. Drink was not one of Mr. Seeper's failings, and although he occasionally liked a glass of beer he took very little.

'Well, if he's met with an accident we shall hear about it,' said the Chief-Inspector. 'There's a conference at ten, Lake, and I want you to attend it.'

The conference had been called by the Chief Constable who controlled that area which embraced Deptford and its environs, and Arnold sat at the big table in the conference room in some trepidation. He was expecting that Chedley would bring up the fact that he had kept the information he had obtained from Nansen concerning Penelope Hayes to himself. But his fears were groundless, for the Chief-Inspector made no mention of the matter.

The murder of Annerly was discussed in detail, and various theories and suggestions were put forward, none of which seemed, to Arnold, very helpful.

When the conference was over he reported to Superintendent Glinder for instructions. Nothing of importance had come in and these consisted merely of ordinary routine work.

Tired and rather sick at heart Arnold collected his crew and set out in the 'Q' car on his ordinary patrol duty. He was terribly worried about Penelope, and it required more than an ordinary effort to concentrate his mind on his job, but he realised that nothing more could be done than was being done. Every department in Scotland Yard had been pressed into service in a search for the missing girl. Her description had been circulated to every police station in the country, and every patrolman was on the lookout for any clue that might lead to the discovery of her whereabouts. No photograph was available, unfortunately, but *'Printed Information'* carried a detailed description of her, and also a paragraph concerning the unknown Clark Quinton, with such meagre details as was known about him.

An attempted 'smash-and-grab' raid lent a little excitement to the day. A man threw a brick, smashing the window of a jeweller's shop in Hammersmith Broadway, and grabbing a tray of expensive rings attempted to make his get-away in a car. Arnold, who was near the spot at the time, gave chase, and the thief and his companions were caught, more dead than alive, after piling their machine up on a lamp standard. Arnold hauled them back to Cannon Row and discovered that there was a message for him at Scotland Yard.

It was from Ernie Williams. The little 'nose' had telephoned to say that he had certain valuable information for him, and would Arnold pick him up on the following night near Holborn Tube Station.

'That's the biggest help we've got,' said

Superintendent Glinder, when he'd relayed this message. 'In my opinion we stand more chance of finding this fellow who's responsible for this crime organisation through Williams than any other way.'

Arnold agreed with him. He knew very well that ninety-per cent of police work was brought to a successful conclusion through 'information received,' generally from the professional 'nose.'

In the vestibule he ran into Chedley just coming in. The Chief-Inspector was tired and inclined to be gloomy.

'No further clues have come to light at all,' he said, in answer to Arnold's question. 'I've interviewed every known person who came in contact with Annerly and they can give me no information whatever regarding the reason for his sojourn in Viddle Street under the name of Barney Gore. The only person who could help us is the girl, and she's vanished. If we could find her I think it would go a long way towards clearing up this murder business.'

Arnold, who was less interested in the murder business than in the welfare of

Penelope, heartily endorsed his Chief's wishes.

'I wish to heaven we could find her!' he said.

'Oh, we'll find her,' answered Chedley. 'But whether she'll be in a position to talk when we do is another matter.'

There was no mistaking the significance of his words, and Arnold, who had been almost afraid to admit the possibility to himself, suppressed a shudder. That was the danger — that when they found Penelope it would be too late.

He went back to his flat a prey to the blackest depression, and the first sound that greeted his ears as he stepped into the little hall was a loud and prolonged snore. It came from the half open door of Mr. Seeper's room, and with a muttered exclamation Arnold went over and peered in.

His servant was lying on the bed fully clothed, and the atmosphere of the little bedroom reeked of whisky.

Arnold's brows contracted, and stooping over the bed he shook the sleeping man roughly by the shoulder Mr. Seeper grunted and opened a bleary eye.

'Wa's a marrer?' he said thickly. 'Go 'way.'

'Where have you been?' demanded Arnold.

'Go 'way,' said Mr. Seeper again. 'Le'me alone.'

Arnold stared down at him in astonishment. The little man was obviously under the influence of drink, was within measureable distance of being drunk!

'You pull yourself together!' he said sternly. 'What do you mean by stopping out all night and then coming home in this disgusting state?'

Mr. Seeper groaned again and opened his eyes.

'Leave me alone,' he said again. 'I'm all right. All I want is to get a little sleep. Go and look after the lady.'

'What the dickens are you talking about?' cried the exasperated and angry Arnold.

'Go and look after the lady,' repeated Mr. Seeper, waving his hand vaguely. 'In your room . . .'

'In my room?' echoed Arnold. 'Do you

309

mean you've brought some woman — '

'Go and look after 'er,' said Mr. Seeper. 'I think she wants 'ttention.'

Arnold uttered an exclamation of disgust.

'I'll talk to you when you're sober!' he snarled, and leaving Mr. Seeper to relapse once more into a heavy sleep hurried along to his own room.

Flinging open the door he switched on the light and got one of the biggest surprises of his life. Curled up on his bed and sleeping peacefully was Penelope Hayes.

# 26

## Penelope Speaks

'She's in a very weak condition,' said the police doctor, coming into Arnold Lake's little sitting room and closing the door. 'Lack of sleep and proper food mostly, I think. I've given her some beef extract and a sedative, and she ought to be all right in the morning. Until then I should strongly advise not disturbing her.'

The Chief Inspector grunted disappointedly. He had hoped that the girl would be in a position to supply him with the information he wanted at once. But he accepted the doctor's edict philosophically. Long service in the police force had taught him patience, if nothing else.

He had come post-haste to the little flat immediately on receiving Arnold Lake's telephone message, for the astounded young inspector, when he had recovered from the shock of his unexpected discovery of Penelope asleep on his own bed, had notified Scotland Yard. It had been at his suggestion that Chedley had brought the doctor with him, for the girl had looked so ill that Arnold had been alarmed.

'You don't think there's anything to worry about?' he asked anxiously.

The doctor shook his head.

'Oh, no,' he said. 'It's nothing serious. Just shock and insufficient nourishment, that's all. She ought to be quite all right after a good sleep.'

'I wonder how she turned up here?' muttered Chedley. 'Obviously your man brought her, but I'd like to know where he found her. Let's have him in and hear his story.'

'We've got to wake him up first,' said Arnold grimly. 'At the best of times that's not an easy job, but in his present state I should say it was next door to a miracle.'

'I thought you said he didn't drink?' remarked the Chief Inspector.

'He doesn't, as a rule,' answered Arnold. 'Perhaps he felt in need of a stimulant when he got here. He had the drink here.' He jerked his head towards a used glass on the sideboard. 'And a pretty stiff one from the look of the decanter. I'll go and see if I can bring him back to his senses.'

He left them, and after a great deal of delay returned, gripping the sleepy-eyed and still dazed Mr. Seeper by the arm.

'Now, then,' he said, as he sat him in the least comfortable chair in the room. 'Let's hear from you! How did you succeed in finding Miss Hayes?'

'Because,' said Mr. Seeper extravagantly, 'I'm the greatest detective that ever lived!'

'That may be,' said Arnold, 'but that doesn't answer my question.'

'I'll tell you the whole story,' said Mr. Seeper, and rather haltingly, interspersed with a great deal of flattering remarks concerning the brilliance of his mental equipment, he proceeded to do so.

'When I'd got the key from this feller,' he concluded. 'I went back to this little hut place and unlocked the door. The girl was a bit scared at first, but I soon succeeded in assuring her that I was a friend, and we thought over what was best to be done. I wanted her to stop where she was while I got in touch with the police, for I could see that she was in a pretty bad state. But she wouldn't hear of it; wouldn't let me leave her. Except that we were somewhere near St. Mary Cray and not very far away from Farnborough I didn't know where we was. She was frightened that some feller she called Clark Quinton would come along before we could get away, and to quieten her I suggested we should chance our luck and try and find our way to St. Mary Cray. We wandered about for hours. It was dark and there was nobody to ask. We must 'ave walked miles and the girl was getting pretty well knocked up. At last, however, we came to a little village. It wasn't St. Mary Cray, but after them lanes and fields it was like 'eaven to see an 'ouse. It was getting light by now, and perishing cold. I wasn't feeling so good meself and Miss What's-her-name was all in. I didn't like to knock at any of the cottages 'cause by this time we must 'ave looked like a couple of tramps. We was nearly droppin' when we found a sort of barn place standin' in a field, and I said, 'What about 'aving a rest until it was light?' To cut a long story short we decided to do this, and I went over and busted the padlock and we made ourselves as comfortable as we could inside. I'd already told the lady who I was, and she seemed to know you, sir' — he glanced at Arnold — 'and said would I ring you up first thing in the morning and it'd be all right.

'Well, we was pretty well tired out when we reached this barn and we both fell asleep, and when I woke up again it was broad daylight. I looked at me watch and found it was after three in the afternoon. I woke Miss Thing-a-me-bob and told her it weren't no good ringing you up then 'cause you'd probably be out, and even if I rang up the Yard you wouldn't get the message till you got back. And then it occurred to me that it'd be a good idea if she came back to the flat with me. We found somebody who directed us to St. Mary Cray Station, got a train and took a taxi from Charing Cross. In spite of our sleep we was both feelin' pretty tired when we got 'ere. I made 'er a cup of tea and told 'er to go and lie down in your room because she was complaining of feeling sick and faint. I wanted her to 'ave some food, but she wouldn't; said she couldn't touch nothin'. I wasn't feeling so well meself, and I thought perhaps a drop of whisky would pull me round, so I 'ad a drink and went to lie down. And that's all I remember till you woke me up.'

'You've done very well, Seeper,' said Arnold. 'Though I think it would have been better if you'd let that whisky alone.'

'So do I, sir,' said the servant ruefully, rubbing his throbbing head.

Chief Inspector Chedley began to question him concerning the whereabouts of the poultry farm, and this he answered to the best of his ability.

'I'll tell the Yard to get on to the Farnborough police at once, and we can have those people rounded up,' he said, turning to Arnold. 'I'll use your 'phone.'

He crossed to the instrument, and calling the Yard issued his instructions.

'That's all we can do for the time being,' he said hanging up the receiver.

'When this girl wakes up we can get her story. Give me a ring as soon as she's in a fit state to be questioned, will you?'

Arnold promised, and he took his leave, accompanied by the police doctor.

Mr. Seeper was showing distinct signs of going to sleep again when Arnold ordered him off to bed. The servant protested.

'What about you, sir?' he demanded. 'You better 'ave my bed, 'adn't you?'

But Arnold wouldn't hear of this. The man had been through a pretty strenuous time and deserved his sleep. He packed him off, took a peep at the girl who was sleeping soundly covered by an eiderdown, and made himself as comfortable as he could on the settee in the sitting room. His relief since Penelope was safe was so great that he slept dreamlessly, and never woke until the voice of Mr. Seeper aroused him, and he discovered that worthy man standing by his improvised bed with a cup of tea. He found that the time was half past nine, and enquired how Penelope was.

'I haven't disturbed her, sir,' said the

little man. 'I thought perhaps it was better she should have her sleep out.'

Arnold agreed with him, and swallowing the hot tea got up and made his way to the bathroom.

He felt better when he had shaved and had a cold tub. The fragrant scent of grilled bacon assailed his nostrils and he found the table laid for breakfast when he returned to the sitting room.

'Miss What's-her-name's awake, sir,' said Mr. Seeper. 'I've just taken her a cup of tea.'

Arnold hastily made his way to his bedroom. Knocking, he called softly.

'Can I come in?'

'Yes, come in,' answered the voice of Penelope, and entering, he saw that she was sitting up in the bed drinking the tea which Mr. Seeper had provided.

She looked pale and ill.

'How do you feel?' he asked anxiously.

'Much better,' she answered, and wrinkling her nose: 'Is that bacon I can smell?'

'It is,' said Arnold. 'Are you hungry?'

'I'm ravenous,' she declared. 'I believe I

could eat an entire pig.'

'I'll have some breakfast sent in to you,' he began, but she stopped him.

'I'd rather get up,' she said. 'If I could have a wash . . . '

'Of course you can have a wash,' he said. 'You can have anything we've got in the flat! I'll tell Seeper to turn a bath on for you.'

She thanked him gratefully, and he left her.

Twenty minutes later she entered the sitting room, looking more like her old self. He refrained from questioning her until they had finished breakfast, and then, as she refilled his cup and accepted the cigarette he offered he looked at her with a smile.

'Now, young lady,' he said, 'you've caused me more uneasiness and worry than anyone I've ever met.'

'Were you very worried?' she asked quickly.

'I've never been so worried before in my life,' he declared truthfully. 'When I called at the Park Hotel and the manager told me you hadn't been back all night I knew something serious had happened, and then, when we discovered that Annerly had been murdered — '

'Murdered? Mr. Annerly?' Her voice was sharp and shrill.

He nodded, and told her of his discovery of the letter in her room and his subsequent visit to Viddle Street, and what he had found there. She was terribly shocked.

'So he was right,' she murmured. 'He *did* discover something.'

'He found Quinton,' said Arnold, 'and was killed because of it.'

'What do you know about Quinton?' she whispered.

'Nothing,' he replied. 'Except what you've told me.'

'I?' her eyes were wide. 'I haven't told you anything — '

'You said he was the worst man in the world,' Arnold reminded her, 'and we found notes concerning him among Annerly's effects. There was nothing very helpful, but they showed that the man you had asked him to find was Clark Quinton.'

'That's quite right,' she said in a low voice. 'I did ask him to find him.'

'And he succeeded,' said Arnold. 'I think the best thing you can do, Miss Hayes, is to tell us everything you know.'

She was silent, and he mistook her silence for reluctance.

'We know quite a lot already,' he urged, and then after a momentary hesitation: 'We know all about Marion Hayford.'

She started and the colour left her cheeks.

'You know?' she whispered. 'How did you find out?'

Arnold told her of his meeting with Nansen.

'And did you believe him?' she asked, when he had finished.

'I could do nothing else,' he answered simply. 'He's not the sort of man who would say a thing like that unless he had good grounds. But I was sure there was some mistake. That you would be able to offer an explanation — ' He was a little incoherent and flustered.

She stretched out her hand across the table and touched his.

'Thank you,' she said gratefully, 'you're the first person who has ever shown any faith in me.'

He was embarrassed, and seeing his embarrassment she went on lightly.

'I think you ought to hear the whole story.'

A little diffidently, because he was not quite sure how she would take it, he mentioned his arrangement with Chedley. To his relief she was quite agreeable.

'I think he ought to know, too,' she said. 'Though I didn't want to make the matter public yet, I feel that the death of poor Mr. Annerly has made a difference. If I kept anything back that would be likely to help you find' — she paused — 'the person who killed him,' she went on, 'I should be failing in my duty.'

He rang up Chedley and the Chief Inspector put in an appearance a few minutes later. Arnold introduced him to Penelope Hayes, and after a few preliminary enquiries Chedley came straight to the point.

'Now, Miss Hayes,' he said, 'I should like you to tell me everything you know.'

'Give me a cigarette and I will,' she answered.

Arnold supplied her with one and a light, and leaning back in her chair she began.

# 27

## The Story of Clark Quinton

'I don't want to go into unnecessary details,' she said, 'so I'll try and cut all the unessentials down as much as possible. My father was English and my mother American and I was born in Illinois. My full name is Marion Penelope Hayford, and I changed that, for reasons which you'll understand later, to Penelope Hayes because Hayes was my mother's maiden name. She died when I was about twelve and my father never really recovered from the blow. He was in the Real Estate business and the shock of mother's death left him such a broken man that he began to neglect his business, and by the time I was sixteen money, which had always been plentiful, became very scarce indeed. My father had a great struggle to keep his head above water. I was at college at the time and knew nothing about this until later. My allowance was not curtailed in any way, and during my holidays there seemed to be no lack of money.'

She paused for a moment, and drew thoughtfully at her cigarette.

'I was eighteen when I first met Clark Quinton,' she went on. 'I had come home for the summer vacation and found him staying with father at our house on Long Island. He was not a good looking man, but attractive, and father was full of his praises. He paid me a great deal of attention and I went back to college for my last term completely infatuated.' She reddened a little as she made the confession, and her eyes strayed to Arnold. 'The only excuse I can offer,' she said, 'if any is necessary, is that I was very young and Quinton was the type of man likely to make an impression on any girl. He wrote me several letters and I replied, and we drifted into a more or less continuous correspondence.

'When I left college and came home for good a shock awaited me. Father seemed to have aged years since I last saw him, but although I asked him what was the matter he refused to tell me. It was Quinton who opened my eyes. He told me that father was on the verge of bankruptcy and worse. For years his business had been deteriorating, and, in order to find money, he had appropriated nearly five hundred thousand dollars of the company's funds. Unless this was made good before the end of the year nothing could prevent a criminal prosecution. Naturally I was horrified, and then it was that Quinton made his suggestion.

' 'I am starting a business,' he said, 'and I want a partner. If you are willing to be that partner you can make sufficient money to pay off your father's commitments and a great deal more besides.' I was astonished, for I knew nothing about business and I failed to see how I could be of the least use. 'I'll tell you,' he said, in answer to my question. 'This business I'm contemplating is technically illegal. To be perfectly candid it concerns smuggling.' There were a lot of articles, he said, that paid heavy duties, saccharine, for example. It was a clean method of law breaking. Nobody was hurt but the State. In fact the common people benefited because they could buy it cheaply.

'He was so persuasive that it didn't sound very heinous to me, so I agreed. What he wanted, he said, was a figurehead. Someone who would be the nominal head of the organisation. The Federal Authorities, apparently suspected him, and so he could not openly take charge, but he would supply all the instructions. All I would have to do would be to carry them out. We would go fifty-fifty in the profits, and in next to no time there would be sufficient money to replace the amount my father had embezzled and to enable us to continue to live in the state we had been accustomed to.

'As I say, I was very young, and it all sounded rather wonderful and exciting to me.

'Quinton supplied me with detailed instructions of what I was to do, the people I was to see and everything, and I carried them out.

'For six months everything went

smoothly. Money came pouring in. I paid the various agents who worked for us and handed the balance over to Quinton. It had been arranged between us that at the end of the year we should share out the profits, and these amounted to the respectable sum of nearly two million dollars. But before the end of the year I was arrested and charged with being at the head of the largest dope peddling syndicate in America.

'It gave me a shock, for it was the first I knew that the organisation of which I was the nominal head had had anything to do with dangerous drugs. I had no idea that the saccharine which we were supposed to have been handling was, in reality, cocaine. Somebody had squeaked. The night before the police came for me I had a visit from Quinton. He told me that one of our agents had given me away to the police. I was terrified, but he said nothing very much could happen to me. At the worst I should only get three months, and he would arrange for the finest counsel to defend me. He begged me to say nothing about him, to accept the full responsibility myself.

'It may sound foolish to you, but I agreed, and I agreed for two reasons. One was that I was still infatuated with Quinton — after the share-out we had arranged to be married — and also he very cleverly hinted that if anything came out concerning him he would have, in his evidence, to implicate my father, to say what he knew concerning the money which he had appropriated from the funds of the estate company. My father was seriously ill in hospital. Months of worry had culminated in a nervous breakdown, and the doctors had told me that any serious shock might prove fatal. Quinton promised that he would see that the five hundred thousand dollars was made good if I would keep silent regarding his connection with the organisation. None of the agents had ever seen or heard anything of him. All the business had been done through me, and I was the only person who knew of his existence in connection with our smuggling operations.

'He certainly kept his word regarding a counsel for me, but I had no defence. The evidence against me was overwhelming, and I was sent to prison for five years. Nobody believed me when I told them that I had no idea that the drug we were smuggling was cocaine. You know why that sentence was commuted, and that after two years I was released.

'When I came out I took the name of Penelope Hayes and tried to find Quinton, whom I still believed in, although my faith had been a little shaken when I had learned of the commodity we had been trading in. But he had vanished, and my father had died in the nursing home. I made enquiries and discovered that Quinton had not kept his promise, that the five hundred thousand dollars had never been replaced in the estate company, that a warrant had been issued for the arrest of my father and that this fact, coming to his ears, had brought about his death.'

Her voice trembled a little, but she went on steadily.

'My eyes were opened to the real

character of Quinton then. He had shielded himself behind me and allowed me to suffer for his crimes and vanished with the two million dollars profit which the organisation had netted him. I determined that I would never rest until I found him and forced him to clear my name.

'While I was in prison an aunt of mine had died and left me a legacy. With this money I came to England. It was useless going to the police and telling them my story, for they would never have believed me. I made enquiries concerning the best private agent I could go to and was recommended to Mr. Annerly. I told him the whole of my story. Whether he believed me or not I don't know, but he agreed to take up the case. I had learned that Quinton had come to England and I had a snapshot of him which I showed Mr. Annerly and which I carried in my handbag.'

Arnold uttered an exclamation, and she smiled at him.

'Yes, that's the reason they were so anxious to get it,' she said. 'He knew that

I was after him. Well, that's the whole story. Mr. Annerly worked on the case for nearly four months, and then a few days ago he wrote me the letter which you found in my room at the hotel.'

She crushed out the stub of her cigarette, which had burned down to her fingers, in the saucer of her coffee cup, and Chedley fingered his chin.

'You no longer have this photograph of Quinton?' he asked.

She shook her head.

'No, it was taken with my handbag that night when they tried to kidnap me,' she answered.

'But you can, of course, give me a description of the man?' said the Chief Inspector.

'Yes, I can do that,' said Penelope. 'He's of medium height and very dapper. Always extremely well-dressed, with smooth black hair brushed straight back from his forehead. Rather pale complexion and smallish grey eyes.'

'And Annerly believed he was living in Deptford?' said Arnold.

She nodded.

'Apparently, from his letter to me,' she said. 'That's all I know. I was going down to see Mr. Annerly that night when the man snatched my handbag. He'd been spending a great deal of time at Viddle Street in the name of Barney Gore, hoping that by becoming a resident of the district he would be able to pick up some information.'

'Which apparently he did,' grunted Chedley. 'Poor fellow! Do you mind if I ask you one or two questions, Miss Hayes?'

Without waiting for her permission he began. For over an hour he questioned her closely and then he took his leave. After saying goodbye to Penelope he called Arnold out into the little hall.

'Listen,' he said seriously, 'I shouldn't let that girl go back to the Park Hotel if I were you. Fix her up somewhere where she can be well looked after.'

'You think she's still in danger?' asked Arnold quickly.

'I do,' said the elder man gravely. 'I think she's in the greatest danger. This man Quinton, who appears to be a pretty bad fellow, knows that she is the one person who can identify him, so she is a menace to his safety. If, as I believe, after hearing her story, he's the fellow who's at the bottom of these robberies and this new criminal organisation, he'll try and get her out of the way. He's done so once, and he'll do it again. Get her into some quiet hotel and tell her to register in another name. Let me know where it is and I'll arrange to have the place watched night and day. In the meanwhile I'll have this woman, Fay Langley, pulled in and we may learn something from her. She's a suspected person and she's on the register.'

But here he was doomed to disappointment, for when the two Scotland Yard men who had come to take her arrived at Fay's flat in Kensington they found that the lady had made a hurried departure. Chedley grunted when this was reported to him.

'She was warned directly they discovered the girl had got away from that hut,' he said. 'Same as those people at the farm were warned.' A raid on the little house at

Farnborough had proved abortive for the place was empty. 'Have this Langley woman's description circulated. She won't get very far.'

His words were prophetic. At ten o'clock that night the officer in charge of a Thames Police launch saw something floating just below the surface near Tower Bridge. They pulled the sodden, lifeless thing on board. It was Fay Langley, and her death had not been the result of drowning but had been caused by the knife wound an inch below her left breast.

# 28

## The Gold Robbery

The days that followed were busy and unprofitable ones. Conference after conference was called and weary men worked patiently without any result to reward their labours. Plain clothes detectives in disguise mixed with the underworld of Deptford, their ears strained to catch the slightest word that might put them on the track of the mysterious Clark Quinton.

Penelope Hayes had been installed in a small hotel at Victoria barely a stone's throw from Arnold's flat, and day and night the back and front of the building was kept under observation.

Arnold had waited at Holborn Tube Station for nearly half an hour to keep his appointment with little Ernie Williams, but the 'nose' had not put in an appearance, neither had there been any further word from him. The young inspector concluded that something had gone wrong.

The days passed without result. No further clue had been discovered concerning either the murder of John Annerly or that of Fay Langley. The girl had obviously been on the point of making a getaway, for luggage which was proved to have been hers was found in the cloakroom at Euston Station.

It was a period of quiet, so far as the unknown organisation was concerned. No startling headlines appeared in the newspapers, and no news reached Scotland Yard of any big burglary or attempted burglary.

*   *   *

'These crime gangs don't last,' said a Chief Constable at one of the conferences. 'They've probably had a row amongst themselves and split up.'

Chief Inspector Chedley said nothing. He was by no means as optimistic as his superior. He was less reticent to Arnold.

'You can take it from me,' he said, 'that

337

this is the lull before the storm. Something big's being planned, and before very long we shall hear about it.'

Arnold thought quite a lot of Penelope, for he had made it a condition — a very pleasant one so far as he was concerned — that she should not go out unless she was in his company.

She had registered at the hotel in the name of Fielding and the watchers, who worked in shifts of eight hours, never left their posts. So far as precaution could make her she was safe, and indeed had very little fears.

'I don't think any other attempt will be made,' she confided to Arnold. 'Surely Quinton wouldn't dare.'

Arnold pretended to agree with her, but he was far from feeling so certain himself. The man who had planned the robbery at the Westland Bank and carried out the raid on Cranleigh's was capable of anything.

Penelope learned of the fate of poor Fay Langley with horror. In spite of what the girl had done she had rather liked her.

'I believe she was forced into drugging

338

me,' she said. 'I don't think she was bad really. She struck me as being rather weak, but I believe there was good in her.'

The beginning of the happenings that formed a prelude to the final crisis occurred on Monday the twenty-fourth. Passers-by in the neighbourhood of New Oxford Street one afternoon were startled to see a grey-haired, rather elderly man, suddenly fling himself face downwards in the gutter, while a glass window behind him was shattered. A car, with side curtains drawn, sped on before an alarm could be raised, and Chief Inspector Chedley was helped from the gutter and taken to hospital to have a bad flesh wound dressed.

The would-be assassin who fired from the car used a silenced pistol.

'It was a near thing,' said Chedley. 'I felt the wind of the first bullet and dropped, otherwise they would have got me.'

While out on patrol in the Shadwell district a heavy motor lorry that was coming towards the 'Q' car suddenly appeared to get out of control and charged the car at full speed. It was only a piece of skilful driving on the part of the policeman in charge that saved Arnold and his crew from being badly hurt. The lorry was stopped and the driver questioned. He swore that his steering gear had suddenly gone wrong, and that the whole thing was an accident. The lorry was examined by an expert, and the man's story was borne out when they found that the steering rod had become disconnected.

Arnold, however, was sceptical. Instinct told him that it had been a deliberate attempt to put him out of the running.

He was surprised that no further word had come through from Ernie Williams, and driving along the Broadway on the night following the accident at Shadwell he saw the little 'nose' shuffling past the 'Marquis of Granby.' Passing him he brought the car in to the kerb, and as Ernie drew level called to him softly.

The little man shot him a quick glance and almost imperceptibly shook his head, increased his pace and turned down a side street. Arnold let him go and ordered his driver to move on. He was disappointed, for he would have liked to have had a word with the man. He was curious to know why Williams had telephoned and not kept his appointment.

On the morning of the twenty-seventh, he was called into Superintendent Glinder's office.

'I've got a special job for you, Lake,' said that grey-haired man. 'Listen! The Bank of England are despatching three million pounds worth of gold to Croydon Aerodrome this afternoon. The Treasury are sending it over by air to France at midnight tonight. The gold is leaving the bank's premises at three o'clock, and in view of the rumours concerning this new organisation special precautions are to be taken. Six armed men will accompany the gold lorry and two cars from the mobile branch. You will be in charge of one and Barnes the other. You will form a front and rear guard to the gold convoy. For this occasion you will be provided with arms. Here is an order to the firearms department.' He slipped a slip of paper across the desk and Arnold picked it up.

'Is there any likelihood of there being an attempt on the gold, sir?' he asked.

Glinder shrugged his broad shoulders.

'I shouldn't think so,' he replied. 'But anyway, I don't see how it can be successful. There'll be a guard of fourteen men, six on the lorry itself and four in each car, and they'll all be armed. It will be a very clever man indeed who could get within a hundred yards of that gold.'

'What happens to it when it reaches Croydon?' asked Arnold.

'The six men on the lorry will remain with it until its transit to the plane which is to take it across,' replied Glinder. 'Owing to the weight they're using one of the latest models, and they can only carry two men besides the gold. One of these will be Inspector Weald — I think you know him — and the other the pilot. The six armed men will guard the plane until it actually takes off, and once it's in the air it's pretty safe. Report at the Bank of England at two.'

He made a gesture of dismissal and Arnold took his departure.

Punctually at the time stipulated he

arrived at the Bank of England and entered the big courtyard. The gold lorry was already drawn up by a narrow iron door that communicated with the vaults in which the bullion was stored, and officials of the bank, watched by the six Yard men, were loading the big van with small, square boxes.

Arnold reported to the manager who was in charge of the operations.

'You have your orders I suppose, Inspector?' asked that individual, and he nodded.

Barnes, the man who was in charge of the other 'Q' car that was to form the guard of honour for the gold van, arrived at that moment and Arnold stood chatting to him until the loading operations were completed. When everything was ready the six Yard men climbed into the van, four inside and two in front with the driver. Barnes and his four men led the way in the first 'Q' car a hundred yards in advance of the van, and Arnold, in his machine, brought up the rear.

They reached Croydon Aerodrome without incident of any kind. The gold van was driven into a special yard that had been assigned to receive it, and after the few routine preliminaries had been complied with, Arnold and Inspector Barnes returned to London. They reported to Superintendent Glinder that everything was all right, and set out on their usual patrol.

Arnold had almost forgotten the existence of the gold when he turned into the Yard on the following morning, but he was soon to be reminded of it. That usually staid establishment was in an uproar. Men were hurrying about from various departments, and the whole place presented an air of feverish activity. Arnold saw Chief Inspector Chedley coming down the staircase and button-holed him.

'What's going on, sir?' he asked.

'The balloon's gone up,' grunted Chedley. 'I told you the last few days was the lull before the storm, didn't I? Well, the storm's broken. That aeroplane that left Croydon with the gold for France at midnight last night never arrived. The plane, the pilot and the gold have vanished into thin air. The Chancellor of the Exchequer's nearly had a stroke and the Chief Commissioner is like a bear with a sore head. Unless we can do something quickly to find that bullion the whole country's going to be in an uproar!'

# 29

## The Round Up

It was some time before Arnold succeeded in learning the full facts, for everyone seemed too busy to discuss the matter with him. Eventually, however, he got the story from Superintendent Glinder, who seemed to be the only cheerful man in the building, and with reason, for his department wasn't affected in any way.

'The whole thing was the cleverest piece of work I've ever come across,' he said. 'Both the pilot and Weald, the detective who was to guard the stuff, were impersonated.'

'Impersonated?' echoed Arnold. 'How in the world did they manage that?'

'It was easy enough,' answered Glinder. 'By some means or other the pilot was decoyed away just before the take-off. We don't know how yet because he's not in a fit condition to talk. He was found by a mechanic an hour after the plane had left in a deserted corner of the aerodrome with his head bashed in. Poor Weald never arrived at the aerodrome at all. A patrolling policeman discovered his body in the garden of an empty house between the station and the aerodrome. He'd been clubbed, too, but in his case they'd hit harder and he was dead.'

Arnold gaped in stunned silence. The audacity of the coup had momentarily taken his breath away.

'You mean the robbers merely had to get in the plane and drive away?' he asked.

'That's practically what happened,' replied Glinder. 'They took off under the eyes of six Scotland Yard men and they haven't been seen since.'

Later in the day the unfortunate pilot who was to have taken the gold plane to France recovered consciousness sufficiently long enough to say what had happened to him.

The detective who was to fly with him, and to whom he had been introduced, had called him aside fifteen minutes before they were due to leave. Quite unsuspecting he had gone with the man to have, as he suggested, a final cigarette. They had strolled away chatting to a far corner of the landing-field. Before he could shout or give any alarm two men had suddenly sprung on him out of the darkness, something had come down with stunning force on his head, and he remembered no more until he had recovered consciousness to find himself in a hospital bed.

'So far as Weald was concerned it was easy,' said Chief Inspector Chedley making his report to the Assistant Commissioner. 'The six men who had been chosen to convoy the gold from the bank had been picked from the special branch. Weald came from one of our ordinary departments and they'd never seen the man before. These people knew the train he was travelling by, waited at the station and followed him up to the Aerodrome. On the way they bashed him, pinched his papers of identification, and there you are.'

The Assistant Commissioner shook his head helplessly.

'Something must be done, Chedley,' he said.

'That gold must be found, and at once. There's going to be a terrible outcry over this.'

His words were prophetic. The evening newspapers came out with banner headlines and front page stories. The telephone wires in Whitehall crackled, and confidential minutes passed from the Home Office to Scotland Yard every few seconds or so. The worried Chief Commissioner cancelled a dinner engagement and set himself to try and pacify various irate Government officials who demanded to know what the police force was for.

In the midst of all the excitement there came a telephone message for Arnold from Ernie Williams. The young inspector was talking to Chedley when he was informed that the little 'nose' was on the telephone and the Chief Inspector's face changed.

'For the Lord's sake see what he wants!' he said. 'If he's really rung up with any information it'll be a miracle.'

Arnold hurried to the telephone.

'Is that Mr. Lake?' said the husky voice of the little man. 'Listen, Mr. Lake, I've got some information for you. Real information! Can you see me in a quarter of an hour? Outside the British Museum?'

Arnold glanced at his watch. It was just after half-past nine.

'I'll be there, Ernie,' he said. 'And I hope to goodness you've got hold of something at last.'

'I've got the goods!' said the little 'nose.' 'Just found out the headquarters of this bunch.'

'You mean — ' began Arnold, but the other interrupted him.

'I can't talk to you now,' he said. 'In fifteen minutes outside the British Museum.'

Arnold heard the click as he rang off, and went and reported the conversation to Chedley. The Chief Inspector rubbed the side of his nose.

'Let's hope he means it,' he said. 'If he's really found where these people are operating from it means the beginning of the end.'

He was a worried and harassed man and willing to seize eagerly any straw that was proffered to him.

Arnold came to the iron gates outside the big museum a minute before time. He looked keenly up the deserted streets but there was no sign of Ernie Williams. Dismissing the taxi which had brought him, he lit a cigarette and began to stroll impatiently up and down. It was nearly five minutes to ten when he saw the shuffling form of the man he had come to meet appear from the direction of Tottenham Court Road.

The little 'nose' was nervous, and labouring under intense excitement.

'There's a little coffee shop just round one of these corners,' he said. 'Come in there, Mr. Lake. I can't talk here, and I don't want to be seen.'

He moved so quickly that Arnold found difficulty in keeping pace with him. When they were seated at one of the marble-topped tables in the little café and Arnold had ordered two coffees, Ernie leaned forward.

'I've got an idea I've been followed,' he said. 'That's why I was late, but I think I shook the feller off.' He peered out into the dark street, and then gulped noisily at the hot coffee.

'What's this information you've got?' asked Arnold. 'You really mean you've found the headquarters of this gang?'

The little 'nose' nodded.

'Yes,' he answered. 'If you take a bunch of men and raid the place you'll get most of them tonight.'

'Where is it?' said Arnold eagerly.

'The headquarters of a firm calling themselves the 'Fleet Taxi Company',' said Ernie Williams, and Arnold uttered an exclamation.

It sounded as though the little man was speaking the truth. The men who had been concerned in the raid on Cranleigh's had escaped in a taxi. It had been a Fleet Taxicab which had attempted the abduction of Penelope Hayes. He remembered also that the manager of Cranleigh's had been told about the emeralds in a taxi!

'There's a feller called Ely Sholter,' went on Ernie Williams in a low voice. 'He's at the bottom of the whole business. What I'm tellin' you ought to be worth a good bit, Mr. Lake. I've taken a lot of risks to find it out. If I'm suspected my number's up!'

He looked again nervously over his shoulder.

'If your information is correct you'll be well rewarded,' said Arnold. 'How did you get on to this?'

Ernie finished his coffee and began his story. It was a very ordinary one. He had listened here and listened there. Visited all sorts of dives and cheap public-houses and picked up the information piece by piece.

'There's a vault or something in the garage building,' he said, 'where the stolen property's kept. It's never there longer than twenty-four hours, and they fence the stuff to a man called Weinderg. He's supposed to be an agent. Got a little office near Aldgate.'

'I've heard of him,' said Arnold. 'I've been suspicious of him for a long time.'

He suggested another cup of coffee, but Mr. Williams shook his head vigorously.

'I can't stay,' he whispered. 'I daren't. I don't want to be seen talking to you or I'm finished. Don't come out of the shop with me, I'll go first and you can follow later.'

He bade Arnold a hurried farewell and went shuffling off as fast as his thin legs could carry him.

The young inspector lit a cigarette, waited a few minutes, paid the bill for the coffees and took a taxi back to the Yard.

Chief Inspector Chedley heard his story in silence, and for some seconds after he had finished stared at his blotting pad, a frown on his heavy face.

'It may be all right and it may not,' he said. 'The question is, shall we take the risk?'

'I've never known Williams' information to be wrong, sir,' said Arnold.

'Well, if it is in this case,' said Chedley, 'and we raid an innocent firm there's going to be trouble. Wait here while I see the Assistant Commissioner.'

He left the office and was gone for twenty minutes. When he came back his face was set.

'We're going to act on that information,' he said, 'and if we don't find any evidence heaven help us! You'd better join the raiding party.'

Half an hour later a dozen police cars left the Yard packed with men. They drove over Westminster Bridge and in a long procession came into Waterloo Road. Ten minutes after their arrival at the commodious garage of the Fleet Taxi Company every man jack in the building was detained on suspicion. A yellow-faced and frightened Mr. Sholter was questioned by Chedley himself.

'This is an outrage!' quavered Ely, his lips quivering. 'An outrage, Inspector! I shall most certainly report it in the right quarter.'

'You can do what you like, sir,' said Chedley coldly. 'I want the keys of your safe and I also want to see the vault below this office.'

The yellow in Mr. Sholter's face went a dirty grey.

'You've no right — ' he began, but Chedley had no time to waste in words and interrupted him.

'I've got a Home Office order to search the building,' he said. 'Hand over your keys!'

Mr. Sholter did so reluctantly. In that safe were the instructions he had received from the unknown for the gold robbery, and he knew that once they were seen by the police the game was up.

'Listen here, Inspector,' he said, making up his mind. 'I'll tell you everything. I'm not really to blame for this business. I've only been acting on instructions.'

'Whose?' demanded Chedley.

Mr. Sholter shook his head helplessly.

'I don't know,' he replied. 'I wish I did. I wish I'd never been persuaded to become mixed up in it. I knew it would end in trouble, but I couldn't help myself. I was forced into it, and that ought to go in my favour.'

'Get your counsel to make a point of bringing it up at the trial,' said Chedley roughly. 'Now, let's hear what you've got to say.'

With one of the men Chedley had brought with him taking it down in shorthand, Mr. Sholter began his quavering statement.

'And that's the truth,' he finished. 'If I never move from this spot it's the truth!'

356

The Chief Inspector looked at him disbelievingly. The story he had told sounded almost incredible.

'And you've no idea who this man is?' he asked.

Ely shook his head emphatically.

'Not the least idea,' he said. 'If I had I'd tell you. I wish I'd never had anything to do with it.'

He repeated this a dozen times, but the Chief Inspector wasn't interested.

During the taking of Mr. Sholter's statement his men had been searching the garage, and sufficient evidence was found to convict Sholter and his subordinates a dozen times over.

'What happened to this gold?' asked Chedley, but Mr. Sholter was unable to tell him.

His instructions, which he had passed on to Rawlton, had been to bring the plane down in the grounds of an empty house near Meopham, in Kent, and that was all the information he could offer. Chedley extracted the name of the house from him, and phoned the Yard to get in touch with the County Police and see if there were any signs of the plane at the place he had mentioned.

It was in the small hours of the morning when Mr. Sholter, Billing and a number of other men were brought to Cannon Row. A number of Central Office men had been left at the garage to await the incoming drivers.

'What are you charging me with?' asked Ely Sholter as he was pushed into the steel pen in the charge room of the Police Station that adjoins Scotland Yard.

'Murder!' said Chedley succinctly. 'A woman was taken out of the Thames the other night and you admitted that you arranged with her for the drugging and kidnapping of Miss Hayes.'

Mr. Sholter's face went an unhealthy grey. In his fear and perturbation he had forgotten Fay Langley.

# 30

## Clark Quinton

The news that the plane had been found was telephoned to Scotland Yard at three o'clock. Acting on instructions received from headquarters the local police had visited the Orchard, the name of the empty house which Chedley had extracted from Mr. Sholter, and discovered the plane in the private meadow attached to it. The body of the pilot was lying a few yards away, a bullet through his brain, and the man who had impersonated Weald was close beside him, treated in a like manner. Of the gold there was no sign.

Tracks, however, showed that a heavy vehicle had been driven over the grass to a spot close beside the machine and driven away again. The deeper marks it had left on the return journey showed that it had been more heavily laden than when it had arrived.

When Chedley learned this he got busy. The wires hummed with messages all over the country, instructing the various local police headquarters to search their areas for any traces of the lorry which had taken away the gold. When this had been attended to Chedley leaned back in his chair, weary-eyed and a little haggard.

'If we can find that lorry we'll find Clark Quinton,' he said. 'He's the man who's got the gold, there's not much doubt about that.'

He had scarcely finished speaking when the telephone bell rang, and reaching out his hand he picked up the receiver.

'Hello?' he called, and Arnold saw his face change. 'I'll be along at once. Go back to your posts!' he snapped sharply, and putting the instrument back on its rack got to his feet in one concerted movement. 'Come on!' he said. 'One of the men watching Miss Hayes' hotel has reported that there's something wrong!'

Arnold's heart jumped to his mouth as he followed his superior.

'What's happened?' he asked anxiously.

'Two men started a fight,' said Chedley as he hurried along the corridor, 'a few yards away from the entrance. The two fellows who were watching the front had their attention distracted by this, and the one who's just phoned says that as the men made off at their approach he thought he saw someone slip in through the front entrance of the hotel. Very sensibly he notified me from the public call box at the corner of the street. He's gone back now to join his companion. It may be nothing, but I'm taking no chances. Your car's at the door, isn't it?'

Arnold nodded as they hurried breathlessly down the stairs. The 'Q' car was waiting, its driver at the wheel, and Arnold and Chedley jumped in, the latter giving the police driver an order.

They shot out of the Whitehall entrance, crossed the broad space by the Houses of Parliament and into Victoria Street. As they swung into the street in which Penelope's hotel was situated they heard the shrill wail of police whistles, followed by the sound of shots. A car was moving towards them, and they saw a man run across the road and try to board it. There was a flash and a report from the interior of the car and the man gave a cry and reeling back collapsed, writhing, in the roadway.

'Stop that car!' shouted Chedley. 'Swing across the road!'

The car was coming down the narrow street at a break-neck pace. The driver of the police car daringly tried to block the roadway with the 'Q' car, but the man at the wheel of the oncoming machine drove with the inspiration of desperation. He took the kerb on one side and slithered through, tearing a wing from the police car with a rending crunch of metal. Arnold caught a glimpse of a muffled figure crouched over the wheel, and in the back the pale face of Penelope.

He snapped an order to his driver. The 'Q' car slowed, and under the expert handling of the man at the wheel quickly swung round. But by this time the other car had turned into Victoria Street. They saw it speeding up towards Westminster and gave chase. The magnificent engine of the 'Q' car responded nobly. The distance between it and the fugitive machine was lessening every second, and then from the car in front came a hail of bullets. One of them shattered the windscreen and came perilously close to Arnold's head.

A policeman on the sidewalk jumped into the middle of the road and tried to stop the first car. A bullet carried away his helmet and he leaped back just in time to save himself being run over. The pace was terrific. At the top of Victoria Street they nearly drew level.

'Stop, you fool!' shouted Chedley, but the driver of the other machine took no notice.

Another rain of bullets spattered round them, and Arnold saw that the man at the wheel was driving with one hand and shooting with the other. The police driver gave a groan and slumped sideways in his seat. The 'Q' car zig-zagged erratically and lost speed as the wounded man's foot no longer pressed on the accelerator.

With an exclamation Arnold leaned forward from the back and gripped the wheel. Keeping the car straight with difficulty he shouted to Chedley.

'Shift Kenyon out of the way, will you?'

The Chief Inspector, without replying, gripped the still groaning driver under the arm and lifted him bodily out of the seat. With difficulty, for he had to keep the car straight all the time, Arnold managed to scramble over the back of the front seat and slide behind the wheel. Once more the 'Q' car gathered speed as his foot came down hard on the accelerator but the delay had given their quarry a lead. He shot across Trafalgar Square and into Charing Cross Road.

Up the deserted thoroughfare went the two cars, and then the one in front executed a manœuvre that was totally unexpected. Suddenly, with a screaming of brakes, when the 'Q' car was less than three yards behind, it swung into the kerb and stopped. Completely unprepared for such an action on the part of the quarry Arnold roared past, and was ten yards ahead before he could pull up. As he and Chedley sprang recklessly from the machine they saw a man leave the stationary car and take to his heels down a side turning.

Arnold went in pursuit. The man was running like a hare, but Arnold Lake had been a champion sprinter in his day and rapidly overtook him. The runner glanced quickly over his shoulder, saw that he was being outdistanced and swinging round fired three shots at almost point blank range. But a second before his finger pressed the trigger Arnold ducked and the bullets passed harmlessly over his head. A moment later he had closed with the man and they fell, struggling violently, in the roadway.

The man fought like a demon, and with the strength of desperation. Again and again he strove to get his fingers on Arnold's throat, but the young inspector managed to elude the clutching fingers. He was seeking for an opportunity to apply a ju-jitsu grip from which there was no escape, and presently the opportunity arrived.

With a great effort he twisted free from the other's hold and scrambled to his feet. The other was up almost at the same instant and sprang at him. It gave Arnold the opening he was waiting for. Gripping him by his wrist he jerked the man's arm across his shoulder, stooped, and gave a quick twist. With a groan of pain the other shot over his head and landed in a heap in the gutter, and he remained motionless.

Panting heavily Arnold went over and looked down at him. His head had struck the roadway and he was unconscious, but Arnold was gazing in stupefaction at his face. He thought he must be dreaming. It seemed impossible, and yet it must be true!

With his handkerchief and the other's scarf he bound his ankles and wrists and went back up the street to find Chedley. The inspector was standing by the side of the motionless car, talking to Penelope. The girl was conscious, although her face was deathly white and she looked as if she'd just recovered from a serious illness. She essayed a smile as she caught sight of Arnold.

'You appear to spend your whole time rescuing me,' she said. 'I feel like the

366

heroine in a super-film.'

'Do you feel strong enough to walk?' he asked.

She stared at him.

'Yes, I think so,' she answered. 'Why?'

'I'll tell you in a moment,' he said, and began to help her out of the car.

She was a little dizzy from the chloroform which had been administered to her, but the cold air of the early morning did her good, and after she had walked a few yards, supported between Chedley and Arnold, the dizziness went away.

He led her to the place where he had left the unconscious man and pointed down at him.

'Who is that?' he asked.

She looked, and her face hardened.

'Clark Quinton!' she answered.

'I thought so,' said Arnold. 'I knew him as Ernie Williams!'

# 31

## Penelope Says Yes

It was much later on that portentous morning that Chief Inspector Chedley, Arnold and Penelope gathered in the young inspector's flat. Nearly six hours had passed since the capture of Ernie Williams, or Clark Quinton, to give his real name, and those six hours had been the busiest that Arnold could ever remember.

The man had been removed to the police infirmary at Cannon Row, and the wound in his head attended to by a doctor. It was not serious and he quickly recovered consciousness. His final effort had failed, and he accepted the situation philosophically.

'Well, I've had a good run,' he said, 'and if my luck had lasted I might have been a rich man. The girl was the only danger, and I wanted to make certain of her, but it would have been better, as things turned out, if I'd let well alone.'

He had arranged the fight to draw the attention of the two men on guard while he effected an entrance to the private hotel that housed Penelope Hayes with a duplicate key. He made his way to the girl's bedroom, and before she was fully awake had chloroformed her, carried her down the stairs and out to the car which was waiting.

'I suppose I was over-confident,' he said. 'But I thought I could get away from those two fellows easily. I'd no idea one of them had seen me slip into the place and telephoned to you.'

'What have you done with this gold?' asked Chedley, and Quinton grinned.

'You'll find it in the garage of a house called Broadlawns,' he answered. 'It's a few miles beyond Bromley. I've been living there all the time in the name of Ronald Hailsham. Now, for God's sake let me rest! My head's throbbing like a steam engine!'

'And that's that!' said the Chief Inspector as he sipped the scalding coffee that Mr. Seeper had hastily prepared for them. 'The whole thing's over and done with, and you can congratulate yourself, young lady, on a narrow escape.'

'I think I can,' said Penelope smiling. 'And I'm really very grateful for the care you've taken of me.' She addressed Chedley but her eyes were on Arnold.

'This fellow Quinton, or Williams, or whatever his name was,' said the big inspector, 'was a clever fellow. He must have a genius for organisation. Some of the things that were discovered at the garage were amazing. If he hadn't had a criminal kink he might have made a fortune in legitimate business.'

'Why did he pose as Ernie Williams?' asked the girl.

'That, I think,' answered Chedley, 'was one of his most brilliant ideas. He invented the character of Williams to enable him to keep in touch with the police, and also to become fully acquainted with the class from which he eventually picked his employees. He must have had this idea of a criminal organisation in his mind for a long time, and gone to work systematically. As Ernie Williams he was able to learn all he wanted to know about the people he subsequently engaged to help him, and not only that, it prepared the way for his final coup.'

'How do you mean?' asked Penelope.

'Well, when he squeaked on Sholter he did so with a purpose,' answered the Chief Inspector. 'I've seen Sholter, and apparently it had been arranged to pack up after the gold robbery. Sholter had been promised a percentage of that, and to avoid having to part with any of the loot Quinton gave him away. Sholter and the other men at the garage, too, offered a sop for the police. The fact that they had succeeded in capturing the chief of staff and the majority of the gang would lessen their attention to the shadowy personality who'd been the main mover in the business. In fact I think it's doubtful if Quinton thought the police would believe Sholter's story. I believe he was under the impression that we should come to the conclusion that Sholter was the real organiser of the whole business, and that his talk of the man behind, whom he didn't know and had never seen, would be put down to a clever invention on his part to try and shift the blame from his own shoulders.'

'What will happen to him?' asked Penelope in a low voice.

'He'll hang!' answered Chedley shortly. 'So will Sholter. Sholter wasn't actually responsible for the killing of Fay Langley, a fellow called Leeman did that, but he was acting on Sholter's instructions and therefore, in law, Sholter becomes equally as guilty as he. There's no doubt it was Quinton who killed Annerly and also that unfortunate pilot fellow Rawlton, and that man who impersonated Weald. And the day he hangs,' he added, 'will relieve you of a great deal of trouble. While that man was alive you were in danger.'

'I hope you can persuade him to make a confession,' she said. 'I'd like to have my name cleared from the other business.'

'I don't think we shall have much trouble over that,' said Chedley. 'He seems to have accepted his fate, and he's quite amenable.'

In this he was right. Quinton made a

full confession concerning his part in the dope traffic, and finally cleared Penelope of any stigma attached to her from that business.

'Well,' said Chedley looking at his watch, 'there's still a lot to be done and I must be going. You won't require police protection any more, Miss Hayes.'

'I think she'll get it all the same, sir,' put in Arnold quietly. 'For the rest of her life if she likes.'

For the moment Chedley was puzzled, and then his face cleared.

'Oh, I see,' he said, and broke into a slow smile. 'Well, that's for Miss Hayes to say.'

'I think it would be very nice,' said Penelope. 'I've got so used to being looked after by the police that I should feel lost now if there wasn't one of them around.'

'If I was a younger man — ' began the Chief Inspector.

'This is my job, sir,' said Arnold firmly. 'Isn't it, Penelope?'

She looked at him and her eyes were very soft.

'Yes,' she answered.

We do hope that you have enjoyed reading this large print book.

Did you know that all of our titles are available for purchase?

We publish a wide range of high quality large print books including:
**Romances, Mysteries, Classics**
**General Fiction**
**Non Fiction and Westerns**

Special interest titles available in large print are:
**The Little Oxford Dictionary**
**Music Book, Song Book**
**Hymn Book, Service Book**

Also available from us courtesy of Oxford University Press:
**Young Readers' Dictionary**
**(large print edition)**
**Young Readers' Thesaurus**
**(large print edition)**

For further information or a free brochure, please contact us at:
**Ulverscroft Large Print Books Ltd.,**
**The Green, Bradgate Road, Anstey,**
**Leicester, LE7 7FU, England.**
**Tel:** (00 44) 0116 236 4325
**Fax:** (00 44) 0116 234 0205

*Other titles in the*
*Linford Mystery Library:*

## BACK TO THE LEGION

### Gordon Landsborough

The Brotherhood of Tormented Men is comprised of individuals who were prisoners, tortured in the underground cells of secret police in a dozen Arab countries. On a mission, they have crossed continents to rendezvous in the middle of the Sahara. When a travel-stained group of ex-legionnaires comes upon them, that mission should spell death to the men of the Foreign Legion. But death comes to men who accept it, and these legionnaires are fighters who refuse to accept death . . .

# ONLY THE RUTHLESS CAN PLAY

## John Burke

In the city of London, the *Career Development Functions* rooms are situated on the tenth floor of International Synthetics. There, people undergo the 'Fifth Executive Course'. The participants expect a gruelling challenge — one in which men fight for power — knowing that the going will be tough. But they don't expect one of their members to die in gruesome circumstances. So, is this a test of their reactions — or the insane ambitions of one of their own number?